Se

Severed MC Book One

by

K.T. Fisher

and

Ava Manello

with love
Ava Manello ♡

Lots of Love
K.T Fisher x

Copyright

K.T. Fisher and Ava Manello
Severed Angel

© 2014, K.T. Fisher and Ava Manello

First Published 2014 by KBK Publishing

ISBN-13: 978-1497412217

ISBN-10: 1497412218

Dedication

To Diane, our third musketeer, who shares our passion for books, is our BFF across the pond, and keeps us sane on days when it's all going wrong. We love you girl.

To Elle, our adopted Australian mother, who showed us the path to follow, we're indebted to you.

Contents

Dedication 3

Contents...4

Chapter One 6

Chapter Two 14

Chapter Three..18

Chapter Four..24

Chapter Five 31

Chapter Six..38

Chapter Seven...44

Chapter Eight...52

Chapter Nine..57

Chapter Ten..62

Chapter Eleven 68

Chapter Twelve..74

Chapter Thirteen..80

Chapter Fourteen 92

Chapter Fifteen...103

Chapter Sixteen 115

Chapter Seventeen...123

Chapter Eighteen..133

Chapter Nineteen 139

Chapter Twenty 146

Chapter Twenty One 152

Chapter Twenty Two 155

Chapter Twenty Three...160

Chapter Twenty Four...167

Chapter Twenty Five 174

Chapter Twenty Six 181

Epilogue..187

Acknowledgements 189

About K.T Fisher..190

About Ava Manello 191

Chapter One

Eve

Sitting in the hire car I breathe a sigh of relief. Thank God I'm finally in Australia. I've spent the last twenty hours sitting on a plane next to a man who would rather stare at my breasts during the flight than talk to his newly-wed wife. It was exhausting. I managed to sleep through most of it, or caught up on some much needed reading, but right now I really need a shower and a bed.

I knew I wanted the silver convertible as soon as I saw it out front at the rental office. What can I say? I've always lusted after one. Apparently, according to the chubby salesman, it's a Holden Astra convertible, I don't care what it's called, it looks just perfect. He wanted me to hire a Sat Nav but I declined, Teresa sent me directions that I printed off so there's no point. How hard can it be to follow directions anyway? They seem pretty simple to me.

I turn on the radio and start out on the last leg of my journey, smiling to myself at the thought of getting closer to my best friend whom I've really missed. Teresa and I grew up together back home in the UK. When her mother died of cancer her dad wanted to move back to his home country, Australia. Understandable, but that meant that at 18 I was left practically on my own. I've always been a bit of a loner and Teresa has been my best friend since we met at nursery school, her dad Elvis is the closest thing to a father I know. Elvis isn't his real name, it's the nickname his biker club gave him when he first joined them years before he met Teresa's mum on a trip to the UK. My mother wasn't the best growing up, and she's never really been much of a mum to me, but I'm lucky she's a pretty awesome grandma to my daughter Elizabeth.

Teresa and I have kept in touch via Skype since she left six years ago, but it's not the same, especially when my ex, the fucking douche-bag, never liked her and made it pretty obvious, making finding time to talk to her awkward, especially when she was awake while I was sleeping and vice versa.

This trip couldn't have come at a better time. A couple of weeks ago douche-bag packed his shit and left, leaving me a single mum to our beautiful two year old daughter. His reason, he claimed, was that he found me boring and frigid. He was the one who stopped me from doing the things I enjoyed, he never wanted to go out together, and was so fucking controlling I actually thought of suffocating him in his sleep. No lie. Plus he was shit in bed, no wonder he thought I was frigid, I doubt he even knew my clit existed. I honestly don't know why I put up with his crap for so long. Probably because of Elizabeth, but then when he left he said he'd never wanted to be a father and still doesn't. That proves how much of a dick he is. Elizabeth and I are better off without him.

I haven't flown all this way because I've been dumped, I don't give a shit about that. I'm here because my life-long best friend is getting married and I'm her Maid of Honor. I'm so freaking excited, yet I'm sad that my baby couldn't be here to see auntie Tess look like a princess as she walks down the aisle; it would have been too long a flight for her. Besides douche-bag emptied all my savings before he left, meaning I couldn't afford the extra ticket. I'm lucky that Teresa has paid for my ticket as it is, and that my mum is happy to look after Elizabeth, allowing me a full month with my friend.

I haven't met Bill, her soon to be husband, but I have seen some pictures and from what I can see, Teresa is one lucky lady. Bill is hot and I mean really hot, covered in tattoos and leather. I'm a little nervous about meeting him, he's in the same biker club as Elvis. They're called Severed MC, named after the small Australian town I'm heading for. I've never been around a motorcycle club before, but I've read all about them on my Kindle. So because Bill's biker name is Prez I know he is the club president. Thankfully, I'm not going to be around the clubhouse, I'm staying at Teresa and Bill's place away from the compound.

I pull out the crumpled piece of paper from the back pocket of my jeans and lay it on my lap. Teresa sent me strict directions to follow, she was really insistent about it for some reason, I'm not allowed to go exploring without her. Like that's going to happen. I can get lost in my home town, so I'm not about to get lost in a strange country. There was one rule of hers I wasn't following though and that was her request for me to stay in a bed and breakfast tonight. She told me to rest and she, Bill and Elvis would come and collect me in the morning. I'm not going to do that, as much as I want a shower and a bed right now, I'm too eager to see her so I drive right past. There's a little map on the directions she sent me, so I should be fine.

I laugh to myself when I hear the song on the radio, it's one of my favorites, I turn it up and sing along off tune, it's The Proclaimers *500 miles*. It's kind of fitting right now.

***

I turn the volume back down when the song finishes. That was so much fun, it's the kind of stupid thing I used to do with Teresa.

I see a right turn coming up, but I don't see any road signs to tell me which way Severed is, I glance down at the map on my lap and find it's gone. Shit! I look around as best I can whilst still driving but I come up empty. I pull over to the side of the desert road to have a better look, but still nothing. "Fuck!" I scream into the silence. Of course a piece of paper is going to fly away while I'm driving a convertible. So stupid.

I lean my head on the steering wheel in frustration and, after a couple of minutes of feeling sorry for myself, I fish out my phone from my bag to call Teresa. All I get is the dial tone so I try again, but she doesn't answer. What the fuck do I do? I should have listened and stayed at the bed and breakfast. It's getting dark and I'm scared I'll be worse off if I try and remember the way I came.

I stare at the road in front of me, do I go straight or turn right? Shall I risk it or do I stay here?

Fuck it, I'm going to risk going straight ahead, but before I do, I try Teresa one more time. No answer, so I leave her a voice mail. "Hey Tess, I'm here. I didn't stay at the bed and breakfast though, I was so desperate to see you I carried on driving, but the directions with the map you sent flew out the window while I was driving and now I'm lost. Before you say anything, I know I'm a fucking idiot. So now I'm faced with a turn, straight or right? I've chosen to drive straight, so fingers crossed I'll be with you soon. Ring me as soon as possible."

I take a deep breath and drive, hoping that I'm doing the right thing. I have to keep driving, I don't want to sit here alone in my car while it gets dark outside, in the middle of nowhere. I drive more slowly this time and notice my surroundings, there's not much around here, but it sure is beautiful. I drive for another half hour before I see a little building in front. As I get closer I can see it's a small convenience store, it looks a little run down and rustic, but fits in well around here. I'm really thirsty, so I decide to run in for a drink and ask for directions. I pull out my phone and leave Teresa yet another voice mail, letting her know where I am and that I'm going inside to ask for directions.

Grabbing my bag I lock up the car, not that there's anyone in sight to steal it, and take a deep breath before I enter the store. I don't know why I feel so nervous, what could happen to make the situation any worse than it is right now?

I check my phone to see if Teresa has at least left me a text message, but all I see is a black screen. Just great. My phone has died on me, that's just fucking perfect.

Slowly pushing open the shop's door and entering, I immediately feel cooler from the air con. It's so hot outside, I'm tempted to stay in here until I hear from Teresa. Maybe I should, now that my phone has died, and I told her I was here in my last message.

I can't see anyone behind the counter or walking around the aisles, maybe they're on their break. I browse the items while I wait for them to return, picking out some snacks and drinks, dropping them on the counter ready to pay. I suddenly hear loud male voices, they sound like they're coming from the back room of the store. Curiosity gets the better of me and I start to drift to the slightly parted door where the shouting is coming from. I peek though the gap as quietly as I can and see three men wearing leather vests. They have their backs facing me so I can see the words Carnal MC written on the back. These guys aren't part of Teresa's old man's club and I'm getting a vibe that this situation isn't a good one. The three men are looking down on a man, head bowed and kneeling in front of them, he looks petrified, and the longer I watch I can see he's in pain. It's dark in there, but I can see puddles of blood on the floor. What the fuck have I walked in on?

The man on the floor is begging for another chance, something about being sorry for not paying his protection money, and he keeps on repeating how sorry he is. The biker standing in the middle of the group shakes his head, slowly, and the beaten man on the floor widens his eyes in terror.

"You've had enough chances Frank. You know my Prez, Scalp, right?" The man named Frank quickly nods his head. "Well he said either you pay or your wife and kids do, so which is it Frank?"

Frank starts to cry. "Please don't hurt them Satan, this is my problem, leave them out of it."

"Well that was easy Frank." Without another thought I see the man named Satan, although I'm sure that's not his actual name, lift his right arm. A loud bang fills the store, making me jump. The back of Frank's head is covered in blood and he falls face first onto the floor, right at the biker's feet. One of the bikers turns around and spots me, I gasp causing the other two to turn and see me also. I slowly back up, I need to get out of here. What a brilliant idea it was to come in here - not. I should have fucking stayed where I was half an hour ago.

My back hits something solid, I really don't want to look over my shoulder because I have a terrible feeling I know what's behind me. Turning my head anyway, I scream when I see the huge hairy biker standing there. He looks terrifying and I start to run away but he captures me in his arms. "Not so fast." He holds me tight against him, I'm pretty certain I can feel his erection digging in my back. Eeeww. "Pretty little thing ain't you girl?" I struggle, trying to get out of his arms. "Let me go. Please."

Big hairy biker laughs behind me. "You hearing her Satan? Posh little bitch here wants to go."

Posh? I'm not fucking posh.

The other three walk through the door to stand facing me. They're all attractive but the one called Satan is the better looking one, he'd look even hotter if he didn't look so scary and have a permanent scowl. These bikers are not good guys at all. "Why are you here?" Satan growls at me.

"I-I just wanted a drink."

He cruelly smirks. "Get on your knees and I can personally give you a drink." I silently gag. "No thanks."

They all laugh, the man holding me pushes his erection into my back. Satan takes a step closer and looks me up and down. "You sound British, what are you doing here?" I don't want to answer him so I clench my jaw. He takes another step forward and slaps me across the face. It's so hard my head snaps to the side and I cry out, it burns and brings tears to my eyes. "Answer me bitch."

"To see a friend."

"Well, who has a pretty little girl like you as a friend?"

I don't want to tell them Teresa's name. Satan's eyes wander over me some more, lingering on my breasts. The biker behind me squeezes me harder, reminding me to answer. "Just an old friend."

Satan wraps his hand around my throat and squeezes, making it hard to breathe. "I want names."

"Severed." I answer, my voice sounding strained. I didn't want to say Teresa or Bill's names, so I said where I was going.

His eyes widen a little and he grabs me, throwing me to the floor. "She's a Severed bitch."

I raise my eyes and see four guns pointing down at me. I look into the barrel of Satan's gun, my life's about to end and I don't experience the flashback people talk about. I think about my beautiful daughter, her cute little face and the way her eyes light up when she smiles at me. *Mummy loves you Elizabeth*, I say to her in my thoughts. A lone tear slides down my cheek as I realize I'm never going to see her again, and I close my eyes.

The rumbling of bikes stops Satan advancing on me and my eyes snap open to see the bikers have lowered their guns. "Fuck it's them, leave now." They all run out of the back door. That explains why I didn't see their bikes when I arrived. Satan gives me one last glare before leaving. "I'll see you next time bitch."

I begin to shake, sitting there alone on the floor. In a state of shock I slowly stand, I really thought I was going to die.

Movement outside the shop windows catches my attention and my eyes widen at the sight of more bikers, the door opens and I see Satan walk back in. I need to escape, quickly turning and running for the room where Frank lays dead on the floor. Shit what am I going to do? Where am I going to go? They've obviously thought better of leaving me alive, they're coming back to kill me. "You alright babe'?"

I turn to see Satan standing in the doorway, I want to run away but my head starts to spin and I scream out as blackness takes over.

Chapter Two

Gabe

As soon as Prez's old lady Teresa started to freak out after listening to her voicemail and her friend wasn't answering the phone, he called in some of the brothers to find her. She should have stuck to the plan and gone straight to the bed and breakfast if you ask me, but no point in bitching about it now. For some reason my gut was telling me this wasn't good, it was more than a case of getting lost, it sounded like she'd strayed into Carnal territory, and they were some crazy fuckers you didn't want to mess with.

I almost laugh when I pull up and see Satan running away on his bike along with his pathetic excuse for brothers. Luckily there are more of us than them or I'm damned certain he'd have stayed and shot it out. Carnal don't know the true meaning of a brother in an MC. They'd turn their backs on one of their own for pussy or money, and not think anything of stabbing him in the back, both figuratively and literally. Trust me, I know.

I step into the store and see a girl run into the back. While my brothers check out what Carnal have been up to, I decide to follow her. I stop in the doorway looking around, there's blood everywhere and Frank, the shop owner, lays dead on the floor. What is Satan thinking? Killing innocent people and in front of a woman. That's the problem though, Satan doesn't think.

I look at the girl, standing in the midst of this murder scene, she's looking scared shitless but she's easily the sexiest woman I've ever seen. Pretty fucked up that I'm a little turned on right now, I'm hoping she can't see my cock straining against my jeans. I see her start to fall and manage to catch her just as she's about to hit the floor. She lands in my arms, her auburn hair flowing everywhere, eyes closed and her full lips slightly open.

"What the fuck happened?" I look up from my daze to see my club brother Dragon glaring down at me.

Prez walks in right after, looks down at us and laughs. "She's fucking fainted at the sight of you. Told you you're a scary looking fucker."

Dragon steps closer as Ink and Disney walk in. Dragon decides to act like a damsel and screeches with his hand on his forehead, "Oh Angel, you're so good looking I'm gonna faint."

The guys laugh but I'm not in the mood. "Shut the fuck up, go get her keys. We need to get out of here."

Disney leaves, grumbling about some shit, and Ink steps forward. "Elvis is on his way with the truck for the girl."

I shake my head. "I'm taking her in the car, Elvis can load my bike."

I look up to Prez for approval, he gives me a funny look before nodding his head. "Gotta ring my woman, she's fucking freaking out. Want her at the compound where she's safe from those fuckers"

I effortlessly pick up the girl, following them all out of this shit hole of a store. I lay the girl in the back of the car and shut her in. Elvis comes running towards me from the truck he just pulled up in. He looks towards the car and back to me. "How is she?"

"She's fine. Probably a good idea to put her on lockdown. You know what he's like, he doesn't stand for witnesses watching his shit."

"This was Satan?"

"He drove off as we pulled up. If I didn't know it was him, the look on the girl's face when she saw me would have been proof enough."

He huffs and nods his head. "Take care of her, she's like a second daughter to me."

I nod. "Got it." At Severed we respect women, even the club whores get more respect than they would elsewhere, but old ladies and club members' daughters are special.

"Oh and Angel? Her name's Eve, don't be calling her girl again."

I nod, even though as VP I rank higher than Elvis, he's been part of the club longer than me and is the son of an original member.

I get in the car, grimacing. I really don't want to be seen driving this girly piece of shit. I watch the boys carefully lift my bike onto the truck. We leave in a convoy to return to the compound. We left Carnal's shit for them to clean up themselves. Frank didn't bother with CCTV so that'll make it easier for them. Eve will be the only loose straw in their clean up.

As I drive with Eve in the back I think about Satan. Carnal MC are as different as you can get from our club. Severed MC was formed by men who loved the biker life and we still have some of the original members and their families as part of the club. We stay within the confines of the law, earning legit money from our businesses. Carnal are the total opposite.

They're all about money and violence. They run drugs, protection rackets, trade weapons and have recently started trafficking women; fucking disgusting.

They are brutal, Severed may be legit but we still know how to look after ourselves. Nobody hurts a Severed member and Elvis has made it clear Eve is part of his family, so we'll protect her the same as one of our own now.

I think about where we stand with Carnal. Does Satan know that Eve is Severed property? If he hurts her he knows we'll retaliate. He doesn't like anyone witnessing his business and I have a feeling she did, hence her reaction to me. That means Satan will be after her, and if Satan's after you, you better be ready. Either way, Eve will have the full protection of the club, and she'll need it if she's going to survive.

On the drive back I contemplate the history between me and Satan, he's my baby brother, and from the moment he could walk he's set out to take anything and everything that I care about. It's as though he has this insane jealousy that I'm the eldest. It came to a head a few years ago when he destroyed my most prized possession and was ostracized by the club. That's when he moved to Carnal, it's as though that club was made for him, he's a VP like me now. He's always been a vicious little shit, the kid you'd find out back of the shed torturing kittens and puppies, the one who'd lie as easily as breathe to get me into trouble, the kid caught smoking dope at the football game.

And the reason Eve freaked out when she saw me? Well, that son of a bitch is my twin, Kellan.

Chapter Three

Eve

I come to with a start, unfamiliar with my surroundings, unable to see much in the dim light of the room. My thoughts come rushing back and I start to panic. I'm lying on a bed, a very comfortable, very large bed, and I'm still dressed in my jeans and shirt. In the shadows I can see a couple of dressers, a bedside table and three doors. My eyes drift to the corner of the room, and I draw in a breath as I see the large, sleeping figure in the chair. I let out a strangled moan, obviously loud enough to wake him. He stands and approaches the bed. "Eve?", he questions nervously.

I know that voice! Launching myself from the bed as fast as I can, I run across the room and throw myself into his arms, bursting into childish tears, needing the warmth and comfort this man can offer. "Elvis. Oh god, I've missed you so much." I sob, his arms drawing me closer to his large chest, comforting me.

"I've missed you too darlin'," he huffs. I step back, taking in the changes since I've last seen him. Elvis is a huge man, not in a muscular way, just heavily built, with a beer belly that enters a room seconds before he does and juts over the top of his waistband. Every inch of his arms and neck is sleeved in colorful tattoos. I suppose, if you didn't know him, his size and image would be pretty scary. I know the real Elvis though, soft as a teddy bear, and a gentle giant to boot.

He leads me back to the bed, encouraging me to sit. The mattress sags as he joins me, still holding me close with his arm around me. "You've got yourself in a hell of a mess darlin'", he looks me over, taking in my travel weary appearance and sighing deeply. "Prez needs to talk to you when you're feeling a bit better. He needs to know what happened so we can work out what to do with you".

He looks sad. I hate that it's me that has put that look on his face. Quiet tears are falling down my face. Even in this quiet room, wrapped safe in Elvis' arms, I can't erase the image that is on constant loop in my brain. The store owner falling dead to the floor, blood pooling everywhere. I start trembling, as the realization hits me, I've witnessed a murder. Elvis draws me even closer, placing a kiss on my forehead. "You're my family darlin', we'll keep you safe, I promise you." I look up at him with weary eyes, I want to believe him, but for the first time in my life I'm not sure he can keep his promise to me. Those men I saw yesterday were deadly, but Elvis is the kind of guy who never makes false promises, his word is his bond, and I hate that I might be the cause of more heartache for him.

"Where's Teresa?", I question while wiping away my tears. "I can't wait to see her". I need my friend.

Elvis laughs. "She's giving Prez shit for putting the two of you on lockdown here at the compound," his whole face lighting up at the mention of his daughter. "She's never been happy living here, that's why they have their own house off compound." That explains the simplicity and coldness of the room. When I saw Elvis I immediately thought we were at Teresa's, but we're at Severed's clubhouse instead. Elvis continues "She's been sitting with you since we brought you back, I offered to sit with you so she could go grab a shower and get something to eat", he looks me over, "talking of which, you hungry darlin?".

I give myself a mental once over, I am hungry, crumpled and weary, but I'm not sure I could stomach food right now, my stomach is turning, making me queasy. Elvis looks at me, understanding without needing words. "Tell you what, you go grab a shower in the bathroom there", he points to the door nearest the window, "and I'll go get you something simple like fruit and water, how's that sound? None of us men eat that shit, just the chicks, so there's plenty of it." I barely nod my head in response. Elvis helps me rise from the bed, guiding me to the bathroom door. "I'll be back soon darlin',".

***

I turn the shower on, turning the temperature up as high as I can stand, needing to scrub the horror of the earlier events from my mind and body. I look for something to wash my hair with. The room obviously belongs to one of the guys as there are no feminine products in sight, just an all in one shower gel with a woodsy pine scent. I hate the stuff, but it will do for now. I step under the stream of water, my back to the shower head, breathing out a small sigh of satisfaction as the warm water caresses my head and the back of my shoulders. I've always loved getting my hair wet in the shower. My douche-bag ex always complained I spent too much time in there, but I didn't give a shit. I love taking a shower. I lather my hair with the shower gel, then scrub my skin red, unable to get the dirty feeling to go away. I'm not gentle, but it doesn't help, I still feel soiled. I rinse my hair and look around the compact bathroom in search of a towel. Great, the guy who lives here has obviously never heard of a bath sheet, I think as I pick up the tiny towel, trying to fasten it around me as best as I can. It hugs my breasts tightly, barely skimming my backside. It will have to do for now, until I find my suitcase. There's no way I'm wearing those dirty clothes again, I want to burn them, they're contaminated by the horror I've witnessed.

I step back into the bedroom, noticing a tray of fruit on the bedside table, a silent thank you to Elvis gracing my lips and I reach for the water gulping it down greedily. I lay back on the white sheets, reaching for an apple, so tired that I fall asleep with the apple in my hand, uneaten.

***

Gabe

I bump into Elvis as he's leaving the kitchen with a tray of fruit and water in his hands. I smirk at the image, it's fucked up. Elvis and water isn't something you expect to see, Elvis toting a couple of six packs is more like it. "Angel," he greets me. "Eve's woken up so I'm just taking her something light", he motions to the tray.

I reach for it, "I'll take it in for you, Prez wants to talk to you. He needs to know what sort of girl she is, how much of this she can handle, and that daughter of yours can't stop cursing at him long enough to give him a sensible answer", I laugh. Prez sure is pussy whipped by his woman, I know he's in love, but fuck, he needs to man up around her.

Elvis passes over the tray, giving me that look of his, the one normally reserved for anyone messing with Teresa. "Go easy on her Angel, she's normally a tough cookie, she's had to be, but this time she's running scared."

I nod, "Don't worry Elvis, I'll look out for her", I call over my shoulder as I head for my room. We'd put Eve in my room, it was the only decent room aside from Prez's. It meant I'd have to bunk with one of the brothers for now, but I guess I could make this small sacrifice.

Receiving no answer to my knock I ease the door open slowly, the sound of the shower coming from the bathroom. I move across the room to place the tray on the bedside table, passing the bathroom door on my way back. I know I shouldn't, but I can't help it. I push the partly open bathroom door a little wider and peek in. Holy fuck! Even with the misty shower glass I can see the outlines of Eve's amazing figure. Pert breasts, firm thighs and a tight ass, I feel myself harden just at the thought of being in that shower with her. I know I should move, but the sight of her rubbing her hands all over that lust-inducing body of hers has me stuck. I can't see much detail, but what I can see is enough for my groin area to be painfully tight. Elvis had made it clear that Eve is like a daughter to him, so this isn't going to happen, I'm not going to lose his respect for a casual fuck and casual is all I can do. I make no promises, that's why I stick to the club whores, they know where they stand. No fucking feelings involved.

Re-adjusting my cock in my jeans I leave the room quietly as I hear Eve turn off the shower.

****

An hour later Elvis and Prez were still in the office, I'd love to be a fly on the wall, but I know any decisions to be made will be discussed in Church, and with the situation being as serious as it is, that will be happening some time soon.

I make my way back to my room to see if Eve needs anything else. Sure I could have sent a prospect, but I can't help it, something about Eve fascinates me. Again there is no answer to my knock so I walk in, it is my room after all. Opening the door I come to a halt at the end of the bed. Fuck!

Eve lays there on her side, naked, tangled in my white sheets, the towel fallen on the floor at the side of the bed. I shut the door behind me so nobody else can see her and stand and stare. She has a grip on the sheet in a tight fist under her chin, the sheets cover her breasts, but leave all her smooth back and ass exposed, one thigh wrapped over the sheet. Her hair is spread out over the pillow. She looks peaceful in her sleep. She's sexy enough to tempt even a saint, and I sure as hell am no saint. My cock is hard, about to bust the zipper on my jeans. This girl is going to kill me, she's so fucking tempting, but I can't go there.

Eve stirs, making a sexual moan. It may have been a sleepy moan, but to my horny ears, it was sexual. Before I can move she opens her eyes, spying me standing at the foot of the bed like a freak. Her eyes open wide with terror and she screams at the top of her lungs making me wince.

Fuck! I wish she'd stop doing that when she sees me.

Chapter Four

Eve

Not long after I started screaming the door bangs open, smashing against the wall, closely followed by Elvis, Prez and Teresa filling the small room. "What the fuck happened?" Elvis shouts, taking in my almost naked figure and the man standing at the foot of the bed.

"It's him. The man with the gun." I manage to stutter, pointing at the man as heaving sobs start to rack my body.

Noticing the sheets are showing more than I'm comfortable with I draw them up closer and clench them tightly against me. "For fucks sake, will you stop screaming every time you see me?" The guy at the foot of the bed says, looking pissed. "I'm not my fucking brother.".

Did he just say brother?

Confusion slows me down enough that I almost miss Teresa moving in to hug me. "It's okay Eve," she soothes, drawing me closer into her. "He's not who you think he is. This is Angel, our VP, you're safe here."

Teresa looks over at the man named Angel with nothing but trust. How can this be? He's the spitting image of the guy called Satan who pointed the gun in my face, he was going to kill me.

Throwing a look of disgust in my direction, he storms out of the room. Teresa answers my thought before I have a chance to voice it. "Angel has a twin, called Kellan. He's known as Satan. It's a long story and it's not my place to tell, but I can tell you that Satan is VP of a club called Carnal MC. They're not good guys Eve, and Satan is one of the worst. He's who you saw at the store, not Angel." She takes a deep breath and looks right into my eyes. "What did he do to you?".

I notice Elvis and Prez move closer to the bed at about the same time I remember that I'm naked beneath the sheet. Teresa notices my flush of embarrassment and turns to her father. "Dad, can you go find Eve's bags for me, I think she might want to get dressed before we have this conversation." She ends on a laugh the bitch. Elvis leaves the room chuckling, he's seen me running around his garden plenty of times practically naked when I was a kid.

Prez moves over to Teresa, kissing her on the cheek. "Bring Eve to my office, we need to know what shit we've got to prepare for." Giving me a silent nod he leaves the room, pulling the door closed behind him. That's when I notice the hole left in the wall from when the door slammed open. Looking in the same direction Teresa laughs easily, "don't worry about it, stuff like that happens around here all the time. You would think they were a bunch of elephants not bikers from the damage they cause."

As Teresa still holds me, it all becomes too much and I break down. I'm crying the ugly cry with great big heaving sobs. I feel like I'm going to break apart and she holds me tighter, murmuring soft gentle words that I cannot hear, but comfort me somehow. We stay that way for what feels like forever until Elvis returns with my luggage. Seeing the state I'm in seems to leave Elvis lost for words, and gently patting me on the shoulder he turns and leaves the room. I get it; he's not a big touchy feely type of man. He leaves the hugging and crying to the girls.

Teresa helps me dress, reaching into my bags and finding me a fresh outfit to wear while I sit still on the bed.

Feeling slightly calmer we set off for the office, and I get my first glimpse of the clubhouse interior. I'm not sure what I expected, probably something more dark and dirty from the books that I read. The corridor outside my room appears bright and clean, with off-white walls reflecting light from windows set in the ceiling. Pictures of motorcycles framed on the walls and posters on doors as we pass, some of women, others of bikes and some with naked women on bikes. A coolness fills the air, but there's no breeze or noise I'd associate with an air con system suggesting it's down to the design of the building. As we walk through a room that looks like a huge living area filled with sofas, a few tables and a huge TV I notice Teresa keeps throwing glances in my direction. Suddenly she stops me and grasps me in a suffocating bear hug. "I can't believe you're finally here," she squeals, almost deafening me. "It's been too long." She's right, it's been six years since I last held my friend. That was a horrible goodbye hug that tore me apart. That day I lost my sister. I can still remember it all.

*"I wish you could come with us Eve, I'm going to miss you so damn much"
Teresa sobbed into my shoulder as we held each other at the airport. Elvis
was watching us from the door that would separate us for six years. I
wasn't sure how I was going to survive without my friend. She'd been there
for me ever since we were babies. Three year old Emily Jackson threw
sand in my face in the nursery playground. Teresa had a fiery temper back
then and I inwardly laugh at the memory of the chubby blonde girl
marching across the yard and punching Emily square in the nose. Her
biker daddy taught her as soon as she could walk to not take shit from
anyone. Teresa was always getting into some sort of trouble as she got
older, but from the moment she punched Emily for me we were the best of
friends. She always had my back, and took me along with her on her
journey to become a rebel.*

I grew up the product of a single mother; being a mum myself I have a lot of respect for single mothers but my mum never wanted a child. I came along when she was too drunk to think about protection on one of her many one night stands. With no maternal instincts, she found it easier to find fault with me than to praise me; she would rather spend time down at the pub with her girls than nurture me. We soon fell into an uneasy truce and I spent as little time as possible at home. She ignored me when I was there anyway. I spent as much time as I could at Teresa's, they were my refuge. I'd spent more time at their house than I had my own growing up. Elvis was the closest thing to a Dad I had, and both he and his wife Babs treated me like a daughter. They knew why I never wanted to be home, I think the whole street knew what kind of woman my mother was.

I was heartbroken when Babs passed away after a long battle with cancer just after our eighteenth birthdays. It wasn't long before Elvis broke the news he was moving back to Australia, taking Teresa with him. I understood he needed to go home, he needed his family. I just didn't know how I'd make it on my own. "We'll keep in touch, I'm sure I'll be able to come visit soon." Yet even as the words left my mouth I knew it wasn't going to happen. I'd just landed my first job, a part time barmaid at the local pub. It wasn't much, not enough to put a roof over my head never mind buy a ticket to Australia. I vowed to save every penny I could towards that dream, I needed my friend so much. I cried the whole way home from the airport. It felt like I'd not just lost Babs but all three of them. When I got home my mother was no comfort at all, reminding me of my dead end job and that I'd never amount to anything and never be anyone. I met douche-bag not long after that and he became my lifeline, until now.

Teresa's squealing draws me back to the present. I'm so excited to see her, but I can't enjoy it, not yet. I've got a sinking feeling that because of me everything is going to change around here and not for the better.

The office looks like any other office to me. A desk, an executive leather chair behind it, two wooden chairs to the front and a worn leather sofa against the far wall. Teresa leads me to the sofa, pulling me down to sit beside her while Prez pulls one of the wooden chairs over and straddles the back of it while he looks at me. "I need to know what happened Eve, I've got an idea but I need you to tell me what you saw so we can work out how to keep you safe." His voice is gentle, not gruff like I'd expected from a biker, his eyes show concern. Not like the eyes from yesterday. Satan's eyes were almost black, no emotion showing at all. I shiver with the memory.

Starting my story with leaving the airport I follow through to the point the gun was pointed in my face. I believed I was going to die right then. I've been as strong as I can up until this point, but the memories of saying goodbye to Elizabeth prove too much, and I break down. I'm so annoyed with myself because I'm not a crier. I either get angry, shout and curse or I'm quiet and retreat, depending on the situation, but I'm not a crier. That would show weakness, and since the day my mother laughed at me for crying over Teresa leaving on that plane, I vowed never to show my tears to anyone again, but my baby girl is my weak spot. She's the only good thing in my life. She *is* my life.

Teresa gently strokes my back, trying to comfort me. When I look up at her I see something has changed on her face, there's a darkness that wasn't there before and if I didn't know my friend better I'd have sworn it was from fear.

Prez has listened to my story in silence, as has Teresa for the most part, other than the odd gasp. He turns to me, regret visible in his eyes. "I won't lie to you Eve, for a start Teresa would have my arse for it, but you deserve the truth." He draws in a deep breath. "You're in one hell of a mess. I don't know how much Teresa's told you about the club but we're basically good guys. As good as we can be, we stay the right side of the law and keep our noses clean. Carnal MC? Well, those guys are just pure evil, not a good bone in any of them. You name it, they're in on it, somehow staying out of jail. Probably have some pansy-assed cop with no backbone on their payroll. The thing is they've never left a witness, as far as we know. No one has testified against them or lived to do so. I've heard the whispers, Carnal have been asking around and ..." He pauses, taking another deep breath before delivering the blow. "They've put a bounty out on you girl." He reaches out his hand and places it on top of Teresa's as he's delivering my death sentence. "It's $250,000, and with that sort of money every man and his dog is going to want to collect."

My brain is frantically trying to process, unable to handle the high number on my head, but I know it's over £100,000. Shit!

I almost want to laugh, for most of my childhood I was told by my mother that I have no value. Well mum, look how wrong you were. I'm the equivalent to a fucking lottery ticket for some drugged out biker. My anger starts to take over. This is good, I can deal with anger. Steeling my gaze I turn to Prez. "So what's the plan? How the fuck do I get out of this mess?" I can see from his face he has no answer. I am terrified, I know those men I saw yesterday were bad news and now they are looking for me.

"That's for us to sort out at Church in the mornin', you girls go get something to eat." He pushes up from the chair, moving back towards his desk, effectively dismissing us. So that's it? I'm told I'm as good as dead and he's got nothing else to say. I'm pissed with his chauvinistic response. Teresa pulls me to my feet, recognizing the change in my demeanor and desperate to get me out of the room before I let loose. Prez seems nice enough now but he's a big guy complete with the whole biker image. He would kill me in an argument for sure.

"Come on sweetie, let's go get something to eat and you can show me photos of that gorgeous girl of yours." I allow her to guide me from the room, allowing her to distract me with showing off my daughter. Any appetite I had has long gone. I'll humor her for now, then later I'll figure out how to get out of this mess. If there's one thing I've learned in my short life it's that no one will step up for me, it's on me now and I'm determined I'm getting home to my baby girl and away from this fucked up situation.

Chapter Five

Eve

I wake with a stretch and a yawn; the room is dark, the clock showing 2:30 in the morning. It takes me a few seconds to realize that it wasn't a dream and I'm actually in Australia with a huge price tag on my head, at risk of being handed over to the spawn of the devil. Then I laugh to myself, devil and Satan, that shit was funny. Maybe I'm going crazy.

The shock of everything combined with jet lag has made me sleep most of the day and now I'm not tired at all.

When Teresa brought me back to the room I've spent most of my stay in so far, we caught up on lost time. She loved all my photos of Elizabeth, but was worried that she's staying with my mum. I can understand her concerns. When I had Elizabeth I think my mum had a reality check, taking a hard look at herself. She's tried to become a better mum, not amazing but better than she was. I think too much happened between us that can't be repaired, but I can't fault her with my daughter. She's amazing with her, the perfect grandma. I'm happy that my daughter has her grandma in her life. Teresa turned the conversation to my ex. She was pissed at what he'd said about me and Elizabeth, asking me to move out here. Seriously? I'm being hunted down and she wants me to stay here? She left when Prez came knocking on the door, demanding his woman come to his room. Seeing as I am on lockdown, Teresa and Prez are staying here too. Teresa filled me in on all things Bill/Prez. She said he acts like a total caveman, especially around the club brothers, and she lets him. I was confused, but she explained he needs to feel like the boss until they get home, that's all her territory, she's the boss then and he knows it. She also gave me a run down on how great her sex life is. Thanks for that, because mine has always been shit and now it's nonexistent. She clued me in on how this life is, all things biker. Including the parties, whores and old ladies. I already had a rough idea because of my trusty books but it was good to hear it from her.

I spot my suitcase in the corner and slowly make my way over to it. I find my denim shorts that I wore before I fell asleep and pull them on once I have my matching underwear on. A must for me, my underwear has to match. I find a clean shirt, pulling it on over my head. Putting my hair up into a messy bun I splash cold water on my face. Feeling a little better I think about what I can do. I have my Kindle but I don't want to read. I send a quick text to my mum asking how my baby is, then decide to have a wander around. I can't sit and wait for Teresa to appear out of Prez's room. After what she told me, I have a feeling that's not going to be until dinner time.

I slowly open my door, trying not to make a sound as I walk down the corridor of bedrooms. I didn't get much of a chance to have a look around when I was with Teresa, so when I walk into the huge living room area I nose around a little. I don't find much, but what I do find makes me stop my snooping; a pair of skimpy knickers and a condom wrapper will do that. At the end of the room there's a large wooden door with the clubs logo carved into it. I push it open to see the room Teresa practically pulled me through earlier. This room looks like the party room, there's a bar along one side with stools. A few tables scattered around, with sofas and booths lining the walls. When Teresa was with me there was music playing and some of the guys and their women were having fun. Not that Teresa gave me a chance to look, she practically ran through here. Deciding not to snoop anymore because of what I found in the last room I walk over to the next door to see what's in there. It's exactly the same as the one I just came through and it's open. I hear a bang and stop. Frozen to the spot I listen for any other sound, hearing nothing I take a peep around the door. It's dark but I can't see anyone.

On the left is the office I was in earlier and right in front are two huge double doors. Taking a quick peek I see a large table in the middle, surrounded by chairs, two sofas lining the back wall. On the wall facing me is a huge picture of the clubs logo, the front of a motorcycle with the words Severed MC along the top and Australia on the bottom. Closing the doors behind me I hear a moan coming from the far end, opposite Prez' office.

I slowly walk in the direction of the noise. I have no idea why, snooping didn't exactly do me any favors the last time. There are a few more doors down here, one door is slightly open and I can tell it's a pool room. There are three pool tables spread around and I find the reason behind the noise.

I've only ever been with one man at a time, in fact I've only ever been with douche-bag, but this girl has three.

My brain races with the possibilities of what three men could do to my body. After reading so many erotica books I've certainly fantasized about the things I've read, but it's nothing compared to actually seeing it happen right in front of you. Where I'm standing is dark, so even if they look up... they won't be able to see me. At least I hope not!

The woman is naked, legs spread wide and laying on her back on the table. One man has his head buried between her thighs, another thrusting his cock deep in her mouth at the edge of the table, and the third is licking her nipples from the other side.

The sight is highly erotic and I'm immediately turned on. My eyes widen when they stop, flipping the girl over, dragging her down the table so one of the men can sit at its edge with her straddling his lap. The others take their positions, one behind her, the other standing above them all, giving the girl perfect access to his hard cock. Her moan fills the room as the three enter her, bumping and thrusting. I fight my own hands, biting on my lip. I am so turned on right now, I don't know what to do with myself. I think about running back to my room and taking care of myself, but I can't turn my eyes away from the scene acting out in front of me.

I catch movement to my side, shocked to see Angel glaring at me. "Like what you see?"

I stare wide eyed, I don't know what to say. I'm embarrassed he's caught me watching. He curses, looking back to the foursome. The girl's moaning becomes louder and I step back. I'm still turned on, my underwear is soaked, even though I'm ashamed at being caught watching. Angel looks at me, snickering before storming into the room. What the fuck is he doing?

"Prospects! What the fuck?" They all freeze, the three men looking scared. I would be too if I was them.

Standing in the middle of the room, in just jeans and his cut, his naked torso revealing muscle and tattoos, Angel looks lethal, more like a fallen angel.

The girl however licks her lips, smiling up at him. "Care to join in Angel?" she purrs.

"Shut the fuck up Lola. You should know better than this." I don't know what's happening but Lola suddenly looks chastised. Angel grabs a piece of clothing and tosses it to her. "Get the fuck dressed and fuck off."

"What?" She screeches. "You can't Angel. Please."

"I don't give a fuck! You've been told too many times. Prez said one more incident and you're out. Well now you're out, so fuck off and don't come back. You know what will happen if you do."

Her eyes widen as she quickly puts on her tiny excuse for a dress before running out the place, gracing me with a dirty look as she passes.

Angel glares at the three men in front of him; it's nice to see they are now decent. "Did you get approval from Prez?" They shake their heads, looking at the floor.

"What the fuck are you playing at?" Angel asks, but they don't answer. He shakes his head, pulling out his phone. He types for a few seconds before putting it away again.

"You know what happens fellas." He doesn't wait for them to say anything, just lands a punch on the closest man. He hits him right in the face, sending him to the floor. I gasp, taking a step back as Angel pounds into him, leaving the prospect groaning on the floor. Just as Angel starts on the second prospect, another man enters the room and joins in, beating the third prospect.

I don't know what to do. What the hell is going on? I'm not stupid enough to try and stop it. When Angel is satisfied he stands and marches over to me. The look on his face is dark, right now he looks so much like Satan that I shrink against the wall. Angel grabs my arm and pulls me, walking me back the way I came.

I gasp. "What are you doing?"

"Why are out of your room?" He growls..

I try and stop him from pulling me but it's useless. "I was bored."

We're in the living area before he speaks again. "Stay in your room at night."

"Why?" He doesn't answer me. "What happened back there? Why did you do that?"

He pushes open the door to my room, roughly pushing me in. "Stay here and don't fucking leave." He slams the door in my face, leaving me alone. I'm left wondering what the fuck just happened.

***

Gabe

Fuck!

I storm away from the room I left her in and go in search of Stacey. I need to get this out of my system.

I spotted Eve wandering around and followed her. When she stopped outside the door of the game room I could see she was getting turned on by something she was watching inside. Her breathing began to quicken, her hands balled into fists at her sides, and she was biting her lip. I know those signs on a woman... Watching her watch them, I have to admit was making me just as horny. I was hard as a rock just seeing that ass in those tiny shorts. But watching her... fuck it was hard stopping myself from shoving her ass against the wall and fucking her. But I can't, I'm not going there! Instead, I beat the shit out of the prospects before taking her back to her room.

Prospects aren't allowed club pussy without permission from Prez. It's a little fucked up game we like to play with them until they patch in. Unless

Prez tells them it's free tonight, or they ask him, they're not allowed. They can go out and find as much pussy outside of the clubhouse as they want, but these fuckers obviously ignored that. I sent Prez a quick text asking him if he'd given permission, and when he replied no, I asked Disney to come and have a little fun.

As for Lola, the brothers are sick of her shit. Always getting prospects into trouble, fucking pissing off the other girls and old ladies and last week Kid found out she's been using. A big rule in our club, no drugs. Weed? That's fine, but nothing stronger.

Club whores are available whenever a brother needs. I make my way to the room they stay in when they're here. I hate this room. It smells of cheap perfume and dirty pussy, but I yank open the door anyway. Stacey is asleep on the bed with two other girls. I reach over, waking her up. She laughs, slapping my ass as I lead her from the room. I take her to the room I've been staying in since Eve arrived, throwing Stacey on the bed. She's naked in seconds, then I'm fucking her. I show no mercy, causing her to scream out my name. Not my birth name, my biker name. No chick is allowed to call me by my birth name, I won't allow it. Stacey isn't who I want under me right now, it's the girl I shouldn't be thinking of while I'm fucking another. But I picture Eve under me while pinching Stacey's nipples. I think of Eve as I pound harder, and it's Eve I see in my mind as I come. I shove Stacey away, telling her to get out. She doesn't bitch about it, she knows how it is.

I still can't get to fucking sleep, Eve is on my mind and won't fucking get out.

Chapter Six

Gabe

I've only been awake half an hour when I get called in by Prez. He wants me in his office, I already know why. My bastard of a twin, Satan. Fucking Satan. He only got the name when I got patched in as Angel, (my given name is Gabriel). Kellan's actions earned him his nickname, Satan, thanks to his fucking evil ways.

I hardly slept, thinking about Eve. She's in my room, in my bed, and it's fucking with my head. I can still see her naked and tangled in my sheets, that fine ass on show. That gave me a hard on all bloody night. At breakfast I almost slammed my fist in a brother's face for talking about her. The guys saw her with Teresa yesterday and, naturally, liked what they saw. She's stunning, I can't have her though, she deserves better than me, not to mention Teresa would cut my cock off with a blunt knife if I touched her, VP or not.

I walk straight into the office, being VP has some advantages. Anyone else would get knocked the fuck out. Prez has his old lady on his lap, smiling at her. He only smiles like that for his woman. Pussy whipped mother fucker. Prez and I grew up together, I love him but boy, he's fucked where that woman is concerned. Seeing me enter, Prez acknowledges me, and then kisses Teresa. "Go see your girl, baby; I need to talk with Angel."

She leaves with a smile, patting my shoulder, shutting the door behind her. "Got a good old lady there Prez."

He grins "Don't I fucking know it." He nods to the chair in front of him. The smile has gone, and he's back to the Prez I know. "Think you know why you're here VP."

I nod. "Satan."

"Any thoughts?"

"He'll do anything to get her Prez."

He curses loudly, slamming his fist on the desk. "I don't fucking know her but my woman loves her, Elvis fucking claimed her as his daughter. She's club family, so this affects us all." I show my agreement. "Any other way Angel?"

I know what he's asking. He wants to see if Satan will let Eve go, drop the bounty without a fight. "No."

He accepts my answer. I know my psycho brother better than anyone. He won't forget about Eve. "I already know, but just lay it on me VP."

I take a deep breath. "He'll do one of two things. Kidnap her, and you know the fucked up shit they'll do to her." He knows. "Or he'll kill her."

He lowers his head to his hands. "Either way, she's dead if he gets her."

I can't disagree. The solution is simple. We need to keep Eve away from Satan. If he gets his hands on her, she's dead, and it won't be painless or quick. "There might be one thing we can do, it's best discussed at Church though."

Prez agrees. "Well fuck."

I laugh as he gives me his shit eating evil grin. If I need to bring it up in church for the club to vote on, it's serious. What I'm going to suggest puts us all at risk.

Truth is I feel protective of this girl, and I don't even fucking know her. I saw the look of terror in her eyes when she thought I was my brother. I don't want her to feel like that again. If I can help it, she won't. I might be risking some of my brother's lives with this crazy ass plan of mine, but it will keep our MC and Eve safe in the long run.

Prez taps his finger on his desk, looking straight at me. "You and the girl?"

"Nothing there Prez." I lie

He shakes his head. "Not asking as your Prez, Gabe. The girl, why?"

Why did I drive her back? Why is she in my room? Why do I not let any of the brothers go and check on her?

"You feeling her?"

"Am I fuck! Look what he did to Beth, ain't going through that shit again." Immediately memories flood me, memories that I've tried to shut away for five years.

I'd just turned 24 when I first laid eyes on her. She was beautiful, wearing a dress covered in flowers. She made my cock hard just looking at her. I arrogantly strolled right up to her. "Hey beautiful, I'm Angel."

She giggled and replied, "hey handsome, I'm Beth."

From then on I was hooked. I'd never been in love, I was getting plenty of pussy but didn't need the emotional shit that went with a relationship. I fell hard for Beth. Whenever Satan saw us together he'd frown or snicker, telling me bitches weren't made to love, they were there to fuck or cook and clean for you. I really don't know how me and him were related, never mind fucking twins. Satan always had a mean streak that only got worse as he got older.

About six months later I was patched in as VP of Severed MC. Satan fucking hated it. He wasn't a patched member of the club but he'd always hung out at the clubhouse. Now that I was VP he stopped showing up.

Not long after becoming VP, Beth told me Satan scared her. I wish I'd listened to her. I should have watched over her more, seen the signs.

The club heard Satan had patched in at Carnal MC. I wasn't surprised. That club was fucking evil, it suited him well. No surprise either when he made VP. I knew he was fucked in the head but I'd hoped he'd grow out of his shit. I was disgusted my brother was involved in a club that carried out the shit they did.

Beth and I had been together a little over a year when it all came to an end. I never saw it coming.

I was out of town with a couple of brothers on club business. I'd left the night before, due to returning the following night. When I left the house we shared, everything was perfect, but when I returned, it was to my worst nightmare.

Beth hadn't answered the phone when I rang to say goodnight. I thought she was already asleep so didn't bother ringing again, not wanting to wake her. The next morning we had to deal with some club shit so I wasn't able to try again. I decided to ring her when I finished and was heading home. We were done and ready to head back when I saw her missed call and a voice message. Playing back the message had me in a cold sweat.

"Hello brother, I'm spending some sweet time with my gorgeous sister-in-law. We're having fun, right Beth?" I heard her screaming in the background. "Anyway, seeing as your club business is more important than answering this call, I'm leaving you this message. If you don't get here by 2:00pm, I'll make sure your pretty Beth finds out why I'm the better brother. See you soon." He laughs, hanging up. I check the time. SHIT! It's 5:00pm. Three fucking hours after I was supposed to be there. He won't hurt her. He can't hurt her. I run to my bike, all the time knowing that, yeah, he fucking would and could.

As I get to my bike I shout to Cowboy and Dragon. "Ring Prez, get the brothers to mine. NOW." They jump straight to it. Just as I straddle my pride and joy, my phone vibrates. It's a number I don't recognize. Opening it I see it's a video message, and immediately feel sick.

I hit play, seeing my beautiful Beth screaming in pain as my fucking brother rapes her from behind. The fucking bastard. She's chained, crying out my name, calling for help. I should have been there. I click the video off as I see another man walk up and start abusing my girl. I can't see her like that. I need to get to her. Racing home with Cowboy and Dragon at my side, the breeze cools off my nervous sweat. Dragon had rung Prez, and they were going straight to mine.

When I got home Prez stood outside my door with some of the other club members. I knew that look, I didn't like it. I raced passed him, but he grabbed hold of me from behind, "You don't wanna go in there Angel." The sympathy in his voice nearly had me.

I pushed past, seeing Doc coming down the stairs. That wasn't good, Doc's a member who used to be a doctor. He lost his license to practice after being accused of killing a pedophile on his ward, overdosing him with drugs. Somehow he was let off, but he's been with us ever since thank fuck! When I saw him walking down my stairs with that horrified look on his face I pushed him out the way and ran up there. I stormed into our room, seeing chains, whips, and blood everywhere. So much blood. It was on every surface. Beth wasn't there so I headed to the bathroom. She was in the bathtub, cold and pale, but once again there's blood everywhere. There are deep ragged wounds on her wrists, neck, stomach and thighs. I look at her hand, spotting the jagged blade, and realize that while Satan may have raped her, Beth chose to end it herself. She was too sweet, and just not strong enough to live with the horror of what had been done to her. Collapsing beside her, I'm on my knees, just staring. I was too late, if only I'd seen the fucking message earlier. I notice the deep wound above her belly button, in the shape of an S. Satan's mark. It's too much. I raise her broken body to my chest, holding her tight, not caring about the blood I'm now covered in, and start screaming. My heart had just been ripped out by my own brother.

I've lived with the guilt of Beth's death ever since. Prez kept telling me it was all Satan, but it's my burden to carry. I should have saved her, she was my old lady.

The sound of Prez clearing his throat snaps me back. His eyebrows raised in question. "I said, you prepared?"

I stand, pulling open the door. "I'm ready for him. I'll fucking kill him, brother or not. It's about time that fucker was gone."

Chapter Seven

Eve

Teresa saved me from sitting in the bedroom, dying of boredom. She charged in, demanding I shift my ass. I was more than happy to agree, and now here I am, sitting on one of the sofas in the main living area. Obviously I'm still in the clubhouse, I'm not allowed out because psycho Satan is after me, as is any other crazy who knows how much I'm worth to him.

The music is playing on the TV creating background noise whilst we're gossiping, the newest topic being bikers nicknames. I didn't realize there was a personal story to each of them "Yeah, Bill's is pretty boring because he was always called Prez, he was born into the life, his old man was Prez before him. Seemed pretty sweet to me, but I'd never let Bill hear me say that."

"So, do I call him Prez or Bill?"

She seems to think for a moment. "Go with Prez, until he says otherwise."

Bill's nickname was tame compared to the rest. I can't stop laughing at some of them, especially Leech who'd gone swimming naked and got out of the creek to find his cock covered in leeches. A man, who Teresa introduces as Ink, strolls over. He's covered in tattoos and is extremely good looking. Who am I kidding, I've never met a sexier group of guys;

they're nearly all hotties. Ink's the in-house tattoo artist and has a shop he works out of in Severed. He's very flirtatious, and has me laughing in no time. He's trying to convince me that I need some art on my virgin skin. It's at this moment, whilst I'm laughing with Teresa and Ink, that Angel strolls over, catching the latter end of the conversation, and looking angry. His eyes fix on me, before turning to Ink who stands close beside me."Catch you later Eve."

I frown, watching him go, then realize Angel is speaking to me.

"Can we talk?"

I gesture to the empty seat beside me. "Sure."

"In private." He crosses his arms, his muscles bulge and I hold my breath for a second. Christ he's sexy. Swallowing hard, I give Teresa a look that tells her I have no clue, before getting up and following Angel. He leads me to the room that is mine for the time being.

He shuts the door behind us and stares at me. This is awkward. "What do you want to talk about?"

"What were you thinking walking around on your own last night?"

"I told you, I was bored."

"You looked pretty entertained to me."

I blush. "So you were spying on me?"

"I'm not the peeping Tom here."

My blush deepens. "If you've come here to insult me, you can leave."

He laughs at me and my anger increases. "Why were you watching anyway?" I don't answer because I'm too embarrassed. "Are you scared by how much it turned you on?" I look behind him so I don't have to look at his face. He laughs again. "Oh, you are."

"What's so funny?" I mutter.

He shakes his head, still laughing.

"You're just jealous because you wish I was watching you." That shuts him up. I don't know where that came from, but I keep going. "Yeah, that's right. That's why you beat those men up. You were jealous that I was watching them." I start to laugh now, Angel clenches his jaw.

"I don't want you so why would I be jealous?"

I'll admit that stung, but something about him tells me he isn't telling the truth. Like the way his eyes keep drifting to my breasts. I take a step forward, suddenly feeling brave. "You wouldn't be able to handle me sweetheart." I purr, close to his face.

He looks down at my mouth, and I look at his. We almost kiss, just a breath apart between our lips. Shit what am I doing? I start to pull back, but Angel places his hand on my waist. "Where are you going?"

My mouth is dry. "I need to get some fresh air."

"You can't go out there without me."

"Why?"

"You're on lockdown, if you're seen you're in danger." His words send a chill through me. "You have to stay safe Eve." His voice growls my name. He looks directly into my eyes, one hand stays on my waist, the other caresses my cheek. My heart begins beating erratically, and my skin erupts in goose bumps. "I can't let him hurt anyone else under my watch." Angel almost sounds defeated.

I'm confused by his words, but I don't think too much. He is so close to me I can feel his breath on me, I'm enveloped in his scent. I love that aroma, it's a mix of musk and motor oil. I could get high on his smell.

He quickly moves away from me, breaking the spell. I breathe again, watching as he walks towards the bathroom. He leaves the door wide open and rips his top over his head, exposing his amazing sculptured back. I have a big thing for a man with a strong back. Angel's back is something else. His muscles ripple as he bends, removing his boots. He has a tribal tattoo along his back, surrounding a Severed MC tattoo. I snap myself out of the daze I'm in from watching Angel strip, and move to close the door, cutting off my view. I breathe a sigh of relief when I can't see him anymore.

I go to sit on the bed and think about what's happening. My life is seriously fucked up right now. I'm sure I nearly kissed Angel, or he nearly kissed me. I wonder what kissing a man like him would be like? The only man I've kissed is douche-bag, and he was shit at everything. He never went down on me, yet expected me to do it for him, and he never gave me an orgasm, I always had to finish myself off. I shudder at the memories.

I'm still sitting on the edge of the bed, facing the bathroom door when it opens. Angel stands there with only a tiny excuse of a towel wrapped low around his hips, a toothbrush in his hand. Oh fuck, he has a six pack leading straight down to a happy trail. His body really does belong to an angel. I know I'm staring, but I can't take my eyes away.

"What are you doing?"

"Having a shower."

"This is my room, go shower some other place."

He steps nearer to me, leaning in close. "No Princess, this is my room. You've been sleeping in my bed." Who does he think I am, fucking Goldilocks? Before I can respond, he turns, dropping the towel on the floor. Letting me see his toned ass, the tattoo stopping just before his dimpled cheeks. Fuck I want a piece of that!

As I'm staring, he steps into the shower and turns it on. I jump up and leave the room. I need a drink.

***

Gabe

I don't know what's happening with me and Eve, but whatever it is, I'm grinning the whole time I'm in the shower.

When I get of out the shower, I plan to tease her some more. I'm a little let down when I find that she's left. I start to panic, she wanted fresh air. What if she's gone outside? She'd be too visible. There's a fence surrounding the compound, with guards minding the gates, but someone could still tell Satan exactly where she is. I quickly dry myself. I can smell Eve in my room, and oddly enough, it doesn't bother me.

Once dressed, I barge through the clubhouse, looking for Eve. Church is starting any minute, and now I'm stuck on a fucking search mission. I walk through the TV room, into the bar. I'm about to head through the main doors when I hear a laugh. It's her laugh. I stop dead in my tracks, turning my head. She's perched on a bar stool, between Ink and Rabbit. She's got a drink in her hands, both men standing close. Too fucking close, and she's laughing at whatever the fuck they're saying. I don't like what I'm feeling inside right now. They can have her, I shouldn't give a fuck, but I do. Fuck, I do give a shit. I don't want them this close to her, I don't want her laughing with them. I watch Eve reach out and squeeze Ink's arm, pouting. It's a show she's putting on, but it still pisses me off.

I've had enough. "Church, boys!" I shout loudly so everyone can hear, even the guys in the TV room. Everyone starts moving, making their way to church.

Eve frowns over at me, and I send a wink in return. Ink, however, looks at me for a second longer than he should before he turns back to Eve, whispers something in her ear, making her laugh again, before walking away.

I look back to Eve before I join the guys, but she's walking into the TV room, drink in hand.

***

I sit in my place, on Prez's right side, he sits at the head of the table. Dragon sits opposite me and the rest of the brothers surround us. All waiting to hear what we're going to say.

Prez bangs his gavel down to start the meeting. "Right we're here to discuss Elvis' adopted daughter, Eve."

Disney's eyebrows shoot up. "Elvis has another daughter?"

"Shut the fuck up Disney." Elvis barks, causing some of the guys to laugh.

Prez silences everyone with a look, "You all know why she's here, but I'm gonna repeat it anyway. Eve is here to be my old lady's Maid of Honor. On her way down here she had a run in with Satan and some of his club members. She witnessed Frank's murder, lucky for her we showed up in time. But, you all know as well as me that ain't the end." He takes a deep breath. "Eve has a $250,000 bounty on her head."

I watch as Elvis curses loudly, slamming his fist on the table. "Mother fucker!"

Dragon already knew this, along with me and Prez. I watch as the other guys take it in. "So what the fuck we gonna do?" Elvis asks.

Ink nods his head. "We have to help her."

I frown. "Obviously. She's fucking club family Ink, or didn't you hear Elvis claimed her as one of his own?"

Everyone stays silent. Smart of them. "I called church because our VP has an idea he wants to put to vote." Prez looks over at me, giving me permission to talk.

"The only way to get this sorted, without killing him, is to set him up." As expected, everyone is quiet. Even Prez. "If anyone's gonna kill him, it will be me, but that piece of shit ain't worth rotting in a cell for. This is the next best thing. We'll set him up, a drugs raid on Carnal turf."

Prez nods his head. "Like it, VP."

The guys around the table agree, and we start to plan.

"I can set up a meet with a cop," Dragon adds. "He's a good guy, went to school with him. He knows we're as straight as we can be. From what his wife told my old lady, they've been trying to get Satan sent down. He'll be happy to help."

"Perfect." Prez beams. "This will mean having to go into their territory to set it up." Asking our guys to go onto Carnal turf is like asking them to sign their own fucking death warrant.

Prez looks around everyone at the table. "Time to vote."

I walk out of church, in need of a strong drink, the vote was unanimous. The plan to set my brother up and send him down is in place. I just hope we all get through this alive.

Chapter Eight

Eve

I never thought I'd be bored of reading my Kindle, but it's finally happened. I've got some great books on here, by some of my favorite authors, but it's just not working for me right now.

I've never been good at being told that I can't do something. Being told I can't go outside is likely to blame for my current mood. Tossing the Kindle gently aside, because it's a treasure to me, I decide to leave the room in search of a distraction.

I sneak around, avoiding some loud club members, hoping I don't bump into Angel and come to what I think is the kitchen. I hear female voices coming from the other side of the door, perhaps some of the old ladies can bring me out of my funk.

Unsure of the protocol around here, I decide to knock before easing the door open and sticking my head into the room. "Hi," I greet tentatively, waiting for an invitation that's quickly offered.

"You must be Eve, come on in sweetie, I'm Sue and this here is Diane." Sue welcomes me.

Sue is probably nearer my mother's age, but unlike my mother she has a kind face. Her hair is almost grey all over, and kept short and swept back.

The look suits her. Her face tells a story, lined and craggy. I can tell this woman has seen plenty of what life has to give, a mixture of good and bad I bet, yet I know somehow that I'm going to hit it off with her. She's dressed in jeans and a casual shirt, a stained apron over the top. Looks like she's the cook around here.

Diane looks lovely, early forties I'm guessing, and slim, her red hair pulled back into a ponytail and totally rocking the biker chick look in tight black jeans, white T-shirt that shows her generous rack and leather boots. Her make-up matches her look, it's stylish biker rather than trashy cheap whore, the only style I've seen around here until now, with the exception of Teresa. Teresa seems to fall somewhere between the two.

Sweeping my gaze around the kitchen I see it looks more industrial than anything. Huge stainless steel appliances, large range cooker and at least two fridges. There's what I'm guessing is a walk in pantry on one side, the centre of the room taken over by steel tables, currently laden with food. "It's a gorgeous day, so the guys are going to light the barbie. We're making everything else in here," Sue tells me. That means I'll probably be seeing Angel today. After yesterday's display and his confusing words I was hoping to avoid him. "Come sit down, tell us about yourself while we get this lot ready."

I ease myself onto a stool at the end of the table, accepting Diane's offer of coffee. I'm suffering caffeine withdrawal. All I've been offered since my arrival is either water or alcohol for some reason. The coffee is hot, black and strong, just the way I like it. Inhaling the aroma I moan with pleasure. The two women turn to look at me, laughing. They obviously share my love of coffee.

"It's lovely to finally meet you," Sue quickly moves over to me, surprising me when she wraps her arms around me in a hug. I look at her as she pulls me back to arms length, smiling at me, then it hits me.

"Sue. As in Elvis's Sue?" I gasp, pulling her back for another hug. From what I've heard from Teresa, Elvis met Sue not long after he returned to Australia. She's not really happy that her dad replaced her mum so quickly, but she said Sue's okay. I don't think she's really given Sue a chance. Whenever we've talked on the phone she's always dropped in a complaint or a moan. I don't think she's fully gotten over her mother's death, and until she does, I don't think she'll be able to accept Sue in her life or her dad's.

"Diane is Dragon's old lady." Sue informs me. I smile at her in greeting. I've not seen much of Dragon, but I know which one he is.

"Why's he called Dragon?" I ask. He was walking around in just his cut last night, and from what I could see, there weren't any dragons tattooed on him. A tattoo would have been my first guess, but all I'd noticed was a wolf's head over his heart.

"He's bloody obsessed with them." Diane mutters, obviously not a trait they have in common. "He's got pictures of them everywhere, including his bike. Fucking irritates the life out of me." She says with a smile.

"So why does he have a tattoo of a wolf?" I question.

"He thought it looked more fierce." Diane offers. "He's got a dragon on his left arm though, and the Grim Reaper on his back." She looks me up and down, appraising me. "Do you have any ink?".

"Not yet. I met Ink yesterday, he's making it his purpose to convert me." I smile. I'm tempted, very tempted, to let him loose. I've wanted a tattoo for a long time now, I even settled on a design, but douche-bag refused to let me have one. Perhaps I should have one done while I'm here, before I go home, it could be my small rebellion. A small fuck you.

Diane must see something in me has changed while I think about my ex. She grabs her coffee, dragging her stool closer to mine. "There's something you're not telling me girl," she smirks. "Spill."

Time passes quickly as I share the tale of growing up with Teresa and her family. Their leaving, and the sorry tale of douche-bag. I watch her face change as I talk, depending on who I'm talking about. I don't dwell too much on douche-bag, he's not worth my breath, but I can't stop talking about Elizabeth once I start, Sue and Diane smiling widely as they listen.

We're interrupted when Elvis enters, sidling up to Sue. His eyes have that puppy dog look as he makes his way over to her. I have a sad little moment where I wish someone would look at me like that someday. Elvis suddenly drops to his knees, breaking out in song. He's singing The Wonder of You. "You daft bugger," Sue laughs, her cheeks slightly pink. She pulls him none too easily to his feet.

"Feed me woman. I am man, I need food." he bellows, grabbing Sue around her waist, causing me to break out in fits of laughter.

God, I've missed this man. "The barbie's ready, get your arses outside, we need feeding." He calls over his shoulder as he exits, leaving three hysterical women in the room behind him.

***

I'm with the women, we've just finished loading the tables out back with the food they'd prepared inside. As I'd walked outside I'd actually had an excited thrill rush through me. Stepping outside into the bright, warm sun, I asked Sue if it was OK because of what Angel had said before. She assured me that because we were all outside, it wouldn't be a problem. I stepped out with a huge smile on my face, enjoying the fresh air.

An awful noise from the front of the compound has everyone stopping what they're doing. It sounds to me like an army of bikes revving their engines full throttle, causing my ears to hurt. The women stay in place, the men spring into action, running to investigate. Shouting starts and, when the loud bang of a gunshot sounds, men who were still drinking and eating drop their things without a thought. Some prospects head over to protect us women.

I follow the noise hesitantly, not sure if I'm allowed around front, or if I can handle whatever has happened. When I approach the gates I gasp as strong arms grab me, pulling me back. It's Elvis. "Go back inside darlin, you don't wanna see this."

He gestures to Sue who quickly comes rushing over. He whispers in her ear, causing a look of shock to appear on her face. Sue springs to action, pulling me to her side, marching us back to the safety of the clubhouse. She's scaring me but for some reason I fear whatever the guys are dealing with outside the gates more. I let her lead me back inside.

Chapter Nine

Gabe

Those fuckers!

Carnal have driven past the compound en masse. I managed to make it in time to see a black van in the middle of the bikes. Slowing down the side door opened, a hidden figure rolling something to the ground, the van then speeding off. The guys watching the gate got a shot off, but it doesn't look like they managed to hit anyone. I'm relieved that we had the barbecue set up out back so they didn't catch sight of Eve, or hurt our women. No, instead they came right up close to the club gates, revving like idiots and spoiling our food. Two rules, don't mess with my family or my food.

I spot Prez already standing at the gates, he looks pissed. Dragon and Disney are looking down at whatever was dumped from the van, and there's a prospect leaning over, throwing up all over the place. What the fuck!

When they see me, they move aside, giving me a view of the body, or what's left of it. On the road lays a bloodied, beaten and naked woman. She's had a rough time, judging by the deep cuts covering her flesh, especially the jagged cut across her throat. It reaches ear to ear it's that fucking long. What is left of her uncut skin is now bruised in shades of black and deep purple. Whatever happened to her had been going on for some time by the look of it. I brave looking at her face and am shocked into silence. Despite the serious bruising on her face and the blood covering one side, there is no doubt in my mind this woman is Lola, the club whore I threw out the other night.

Prez steps closer. "You see her stomach VP?"

Disney moves her slightly with his foot, allowing me to see the mark on her stomach, just above her belly button. The bile rises in my throat, bringing back nightmare memories. The pain feels so fresh. This is Satan's work, the bastard branded Lola with the same fucking mark he left on my Beth.

"What do you think this is about?" Disney asks, covering Lola's body with the sheet she was delivered in.

I look over to Prez, we share a look. "We need to bring our plans forward."

I nod in answer. This message was about Eve, but he ain't fucking getting her.

***

Eve

I'm curled up on the bed, my back as close as I can get to the headboard. My knees drawn tight against my chest. My body is shaking and I can't seem to stop. Diane and Teresa are sitting beside me, their arms around me, trying to calm me, but it's not making any difference. I think they've finally given up trying to get me to talk, I've been silent since I stepped inside this room.

Sue had pulled me into the clubhouse, but I'd already heard the cursing and shouting from the guys outside. I overheard enough to know that the girl I glimpsed laying on the ground dead, before Elvis pulled me away, was the girl I'd seen in the pool room the other night. Somehow this was linked to me. I could tell from their concerned looks, and the way Sue quickly dragged me along without so much as looking at me. I was grateful for the safety and quiet of my room.

So here I am, shaking violently. Tears daring to crawl down my cheeks. I'm not angry anymore, I'm scared. So fucking scared. My situation hits home, this isn't some nightmare scene in one of my books anymore. The murder I witnessed the other day was real. Very real. I might not get out of this alive, the small crumb of comfort I'd found waking up safe here in the clubhouse, has now gone.

Every time I close my eyes, I see her. A bloody, naked mess, strewn on the ground outside the gates. Like she was worth nothing. I wonder *when* that will be me out there, rather than if. I believed I might survive Satan, but seeing what he's done to that girl has shattered any hope I had. I huddle on the bed, terrified I will see him again.

***

Gabe

Doc took Lola somewhere out of sight. Thank fuck. I'm not going anywhere near that body, the guys can handle it. I need to stay here and get that image out of my head. It's not Lola I see out there laying cold on the dirt, it's Beth.

I walk to the bar, asking the prospect on duty for a JD. Knocking it back in one, I welcome the burn as it hits the back of my throat. Slamming the glass on the bar, I'm about to ask for another when Prez calls over to me. "Angel. My office."

I really don't want to do this now. I want to stay here and get shit faced. I want to forget.

Who am I fucking kidding? It's been five long years and I still wake up in a cold sweat some nights. The nightmares of Beth in that bathtub burn me.

When I reach the office, Doc is there ahead of me. I grab a chair, sit astride it and face Prez. He's in front of his computer and holding what looks to be a bloodied USB stick. He's looking at it as if he's not sure what to do. Teresa or one of us guys normally do all this computer shit for him, so he probably doesn't even know what he's holding.

"What's this?" I reach for the USB, loading it into the computer.

"Doc found it, the bastards put it in her mouth." I've never heard Prez sound so defeated before. "They brought her to our doorstep VP. Our own fucking door. Our old ladies are here." He bangs his fist on the desk.

The screen on the computer shows the USB has connected, revealing a single video file. The fuckers have named it *WATCH ME*. I hesitantly click on it, already knowing what we're going to see. I've been on the receiving end of that sick fucker's videos before. The screen flickers to life, showing us Lola's last minutes.

The image is grainy but you can see Lola kneeling on what looks to be a dirty warehouse floor. She's screaming every time Satan draws yet another cut into her flesh. "I've already told you, she's at the compound." she cries. I should be pissed that she's talked, but I wouldn't expect her to have any loyalty to Eve and, from the look of her body, they'd been torturing her for a few hours.

Satan smirks, twisting the knife a little deeper on the next cut. Lola screams loudly. "I know, but I'm having way too much fun to stop now." The sick fucker is playing with her, laughing at her pain. "You didn't really think I'd let you go did you?" He snickers.

He signals to someone in the background, a couple of his guys come into the picture. Turning to the camera he looks straight at us. "This is for you Angel, my dear brother." He looks back at the men standing by Lola and nods. They approach her as Satan continues. "I want you to remember what we do to Severed women when we get a hold of them."

In the background the two guys rape Lola simultaneously. "Of course, this one's just a whore, so she's not having as much fun as your girl Beth did." He leers. "Here's the deal. I want the girl delivered to my gate by midnight tonight. If I don't get her, then this scene won't be the last. This will happen again and again, it'll be your whores and old ladies until I get her." He pauses. "Choice is yours."

Satan turns, walking back to the group. Lola has passed out, whether from blood loss or fear I can't tell, probably both. He stands behind her, pulls her head back by her hair, grinning at the camera as he cuts her throat. Blood pours from the wound as the video ends.

"Fucking hell." Prez is the first one to speak as the video stops. The last image frozen on the screen. I stare at Satan holding Lola, but for the first time in five years, it's not Beth's face I see. It's Eve's.

Chapter Ten

Eve

Teresa is driving me mad. We're still on lockdown, meaning we've been cooped up in the compound for the best part of a week now. It's getting beyond crazy here. I know how she feels, I'm feeling trapped as much as she is. Although right now, I'm not sure I can handle stepping foot outside of the clubhouse, never mind the front gates.

The guys won't tell us anything about what's going on. They just mutter "club business" whenever we ask and hurry off. Even Prez has remained tight lipped with Teresa. Whatever it is that's going on, it's serious. Since Lola's body was found the guys all seem on high alert. They investigate anything out of place and watch wherever the women go. It's a far cry from the first few days I was here. Everyone seemed laid back, but not any longer. I feel on edge, as if Satan will creep up on me at any minute.

I'm sitting on my bed, technically it's Angel's bed, but I'm not even thinking about that right now. Teresa approaches, grabbing my hand. "Come on, we're getting out of here. I can't stand this." She drags me down the hall to the living area, and I mean she really does drag me, because I don't want to go. I can't stand the thought of stepping outside of this place.

"Prez." She shouts. "Where the fuck are you Prez?" She's making a scene, everyone's looking at her. She's the president's old lady, she should be setting an example and staying calm, but she doesn't really give a shit right now. I try and sneak off, but she grabs my wrist tightly and won't let go.

Elvis walks into the room, drawn by the noise his daughter is creating. "He's out on club business."

"I'm fucking sick of hearing the words club business come out of everyone's mouth." Teresa sulks.

"Me and Eve are off into town. I'm not asking you, I'm telling you what's happening.".

"Darlin, Prez would have my arse if I let you two girls out that front door, never mind the fucking gate." Teresa will not be calmed. She continues ranting for several more minutes, until she sees Angel enter the room. He then becomes the centre of her frustration, she starts in on him with more of the same. Elvis is the one to break first. He never could refuse Teresa anything and it explains why she can be such a bitch sometimes. I love her, don't get me wrong she's my best friend, but this is a girl who's been used to getting her own way for as long as I can remember.

"Fine, but we go with you." Elvis turns to Angel "That okay with you?"

Angel looks anything but happy at the prospect of babysitting us. He rubs his face roughly, sighing loudly. "Grab a couple of prospects. Teresa rides with you. Eve can ride with me." He commands, the look he gives me daring me to argue. I've hardly spoken to him and now I'm expected to ride on the back of his bike.

Teresa squeals in excitement. "Come on Eve, I've got a jacket you can borrow."

Already wearing my jeans and favorite black boots, I let her dress me in one of her many leather jackets.

Did I forget to mention I've never been on the back of a bike before?

This was going to be interesting.

***

We head outside the clubhouse and I start to feel sick. I haven't been out here since Lola was dumped and I want to run back inside. Teresa notices I've stopped and loops her arm through mine. We follow Elvis and Angel, accompanied by the two prospects. I take deep calming breaths as we approach a large wooden building. It looks a little like a large shed. There's a row of bikes already waiting outside, a prospect standing the last bike beside the rest. I know absolutely nothing about bikes, all I can tell is there's a shit load of Harleys and some custom choppers. I'm in love with some of the paint jobs on them. Shiny reds, glossy blacks and lots of chrome shine in the midday sun. Someone obviously takes great care of these bikes. Elvis thanks the prospect for gathering the bikes out front for us and the prospect leaves. I see Teresa jump on the back of her dad's bike with next to no effort at all. How the fuck am I supposed to do that?

Angel grabs my arm, drawing me towards one of the black Harleys. I may know nothing about bikes, but I must admit, this is one sexy looking piece of machinery. He sits astride the bike, before looking over at me impatiently, cocking up one of those sexy eyebrows, yeah even his eyebrows are sexy.

"What the fuck are you waiting on?" He glowers at me. I look at the bike trying to think of a way to get on without making a fool of myself. "Get on Eve, we haven't got all fucking day."

I'm still puzzling about how I'm supposed to do just that when Angel reaches over and grabs me. He almost throws me over the rear seat. Shit! I start to over balance and grab hold of him tightly. I'm surprised that when I grab onto him he curses. I wiggle about to make myself a little more comfortable. I sit back on the seat, putting my feet where I'm told and grab onto the back of his cut. Angel mutters something under his breath that I can't hear over his engine but I do manage to catch "fucking women,"

He reaches back, pulling my arms to rest tightly around his front. I can feel his delicious hard stomach. Shit, this is too close for me. I'm struggling to resist this guy as it is, and being wrapped this tightly around him isn't helping. I'm suddenly hot and bothered. My pussy is so wet, I can feel my knickers are soaked through.

Fuck I didn't expect to feel like this on the back of his bike.

***

Gabe

Why the fuck did I agree to this stupid trip with the girls. Fucking Elvis. Prez will throw a shit fit when he finds out.

I'm so sick of Teresa's fucking whining, it seemed the easiest way to shut her up. All week she's done nothing but fucking moan to anyone who'll listen.

We finally pull up to the store Teresa demanded we go to. I let them know they get half an hour, that's all. Anything they can't do in that time I'll get a fucking prospect to sort out later.

Teresa smirks at me. "There's no way I'm letting a prospect buy my girly shit Angel. I'll be as long as it takes." She storms off into the store, dragging Eve behind her.

Fuck, my cock's still hard from having Eve on the back of my bike. She gripped a little too tightly, but that meant I got to get a real good feel of her squashed against my back. Having her that close really fucking turned me on. More than I'd like to admit. I've got half an hour to calm this raging hard on down before I have to go through it all over again. No doubt, as soon as she's back behind me, I will be hard as steel again. That woman is getting under my skin a little too much lately.

I turn to the prospects. "Watch those two like fucking hawks. You hear me." They nod, following the girls into the store without a word. They know if any harm comes to them under their watch there will be hell to pay.

Elvis and I lean against the bikes, chatting about nothing. Neither of us wanting to talk about the shit situation we're in. There's been too much talk of that lately.

"You do realize Prez is going to have our balls for this." I look at Elvis.

He smirks. "Yep. But I'd rather Prez has my balls than listen to that girl bitch all fucking day." He laughs loudly. I like Elvis, he's one of the longest serving members, if you don't count the time he spent in England with his wife before she died.

The girls finally emerge from the store, arms full of packages and giggling over something. I hear the loud roar of a truck. Looking up I see a black pickup heading towards us at full speed. The back window is down and I notice the glint of a gun barrel visible in the shadows.

"Shit!" I yell "Get down now.".

It all moves so fast I don't really see what happens. One minute the girls are standing in the doorway, the next I'm pulling Eve under me as I hit the ground. I shield her body from anything that could harm her. I look up and see Elvis doing the same with Teresa. Shots continue to sound out.

"Prospects." I shout. They manage to shoot at the truck, but not hit anyone inside.

The truck never stops, spinning its wheels and skidding loudly, it turns at the stoplight. I don't hear shots anymore so I look up and see it's gone. I turn my gaze to Eve below me, her face white. She looks terrified. I do a quick check of her and see she's fine. That's when the screaming starts. A loud, ear piercing scream. I look over and see it's Teresa who's screaming. Her face is red, tears streaming down her face. She's holding Elvis by the shoulders, shaking him violently, but he's not responding. I jump up, pulling Eve with me. I hold her arm as I make my way to Elvis. Teresa shakes him once more and his head rolls back. I freeze. There's a bullet hole right between his eyes.

No! He can't be.

I hear Eve gasp beside me and then her screams join Teresa's.

Chapter Eleven

Gabe

I walk into Church and take my seat beside Prez. Taking a quick look around I see the defeated faces around the table.

Fuck! Satan has done a number on our club. None of the brothers have taken Elvis's death well, it's hit us all hard.

Prez calls the meeting to order by banging his gavel. "This shit stops now! Word on the street is Elvis was taken out by a fucking bounty hunter trying to get Eve. This is on Carnal's head and I want Satan to fucking suffer. My old lady won't stop fucking crying and I need to let her know shit's been handled." There are nods and shouts of agreement around the table. "Talk to me, where we at?"

Dragon looks to me, seeking permission to speak. "I talked to the cop I know. He's had a word with his boss and they're ready at their end. We just need to get the drugs planted and call it in."

Disney voices what we're all thinking. "Why the fuck are we playing games?" He looks around at us all. "Why aren't we riding over there and taking every mother fucking Carnal member out right now?"

Prez looks at him coolly. "Because then the fucker wouldn't suffer. Being behind bars will kill that bastard and if that doesn't, there are enough

Carnal enemies behind bars to do it for us." He pauses. "There's too many eyes on us right now, if we take the fuckers out we're the first place the cops will come. They know what we're up to now anyway. If he's taken down for drugs no one will bat an eye. So that's how it's gonna be, anyone got anything to say?" He looks to Disney who shakes his head. "Good."

Prez is right, as much as we'd all like to take that bastard apart limb by limb, we've got to be smart. I hate that he gets away with a prison cell when Elvis was fucking murdered. Satan may not have been the one to pull the trigger, but he ordered the hit. When he gets sent down I know there will be a long fucking line to finish him and I can't fucking wait.

We spend the next few hours hashing out the plan. We decide that Dragon, Disney and I are the distractions while a couple of the other guys need to get inside the Carnal compound to plant the drugs. It's risky as fuck but this shouldn't come back on us. If we do it right.

Prez looks round the room. "Tomorrow's the funeral, we give Elvis the respect and send off he deserves. Any questions?" There's silence around the table. A few nervous faces, some determined, but no one disagrees.

***

Eve

Teresa hasn't spoken to me since the death of her father. I know she blames me. Fuck, I blame me. It's my fault that Elvis is dead right now. The guilt has almost destroyed me, I'm barely holding on. It may not have been my choice to have left the compound, but there's only me to blame. It should be me they're burying tomorrow. Not Elvis. God I hate to think of him just lying there, thinking about his face not breaking into that huge grin whenever he would see me. I can't stand to not see his face again. I want to have him hold me like he did the first time I woke up in this place. He may not have been my biological dad, but he was in my heart. It doesn't matter how much I'm grieving though, because it's all my fault. The looks I'm getting around here give me that message loud and clear. I know it and so does everyone else. Elvis is dead because of me.

Cautiously I make my way to Elvis and Sue's room. Teresa has ignored me, but I'm hoping Sue will give me a moment. I haven't seen her much either, so I want to check on her more than anything. Tapping hesitantly on the door I listen for any movement. I can hear sobbing on the other side and my guilt doubles from hearing her pain. I hear a shuffling noise and then the door opens. I hardly recognize Sue. Her face is drawn with grief. Huge black circles shadow her eyes and her cheeks are raw from crying. In her hands she is clutching a cut. I recognize it as the one Elvis was wearing when he was shot. God that was awful. One minute Teresa and I were laughing about nothing important, then all hell broke loose.

Sue doesn't acknowledge me, just leaves the door ajar and shuffles back to the bed. I hesitate before entering the room as I wonder what I can possibly say to this broken woman. A fucking apology isn't going to help. It won't bring Elvis back. I move forward anyway, I have to say the words that I need to say.

Dropping to my knees in front of her I reach for her hands. "Sue, I'm so sorry." My voice sounds thick with emotion as I struggle to get the words out.

She looks at me and what I see has me loosening my grip on her hands. Her face, that once looked at me with such kindness, is now twisted with hatred and she begins screaming at me. "Why did you have to come here?" She pushes me away then falls back to the bed, defeated. "If you hadn't come he'd still be here. He would still be alive." Giving me one last hateful look she throws the cut at me. "Get out! I can't stand to see you right now."

Holding the bloody cut in my hands, tears fall down my face. I walk slowly out of Sue's room and she bangs the door shut behind me. I sob as I clutch Elvis's cut to my chest. Elvis is dead because of me and the grief overwhelms me. I don't care where I am or who sees me, I collapse on the floor, letting grief consume me.

***

Gabe

I fucking hate funerals. I'm not an emotional man but funerals are hard, especially when the person who died is as important to me as Elvis was. Today is going to be difficult on all of us. Elvis was an integral part of the club. Everyone liked him. He was larger than life and this club won't be the same without him.

I knock once on Prez' door. "It's time Prez."

The door slowly opens revealing a silent Teresa. She's wearing a black dress with her hair pulled to the back of her head. Her face is white, too white. I hardly recognize her. There's none of her spark left. Standing in front of me is the shell of the woman I know. The death of her dad is proving tough on her. I pull her into my arms. She's stiff and stays silent, rejecting my comfort.

Prez comes out dressed in black jeans, a black button down and his cut. The outfit matching mine. He reaches for Teresa's hand and she takes it. She's moving in slow motion and Prez leads her out. If he hadn't I don't think she would have been capable.

We head out front of the clubhouse, the hearse parked by the entrance. A couple of cars for the women in the middle of a crowd of bikes. Elvis knew a lot of bikers and had stayed with other charters when he travelled around. Those bikers that knew him so well have come to support us today. All of the bikes are lined up at the rear of the cars with Dragons, mine and Prez's bikes at the front of them all in true biker tradition.

Prez helps Teresa into the first car with Sue. I don't see Eve in there. Looks like they're still not speaking to her, which is pretty sad. From what I've seen Eve is hurting just as much. Putting Eve out of my mind I follow Prez to our bikes. We're still on edge with Satan trying to get hold of Eve, but he would be fucking stupid to try anything today with this many bikers around.

Fuck, I wish this day was over with already.

***

Eve

I stand at the back of the crowded church, unsure of my place in the proceedings. I hate funerals. I'm lucky to have only had to endure a few in my life. None of them as close to me as Elvis or hurt this bad. Teresa and Sue still can't bear the sight of me so I came here in a car with some of the other old ladies. They couldn't stand the sight of me either. I sat in silence on the way with my head down, tears dripping down my face.

The minister is talking, but I haven't a clue what he's saying. The coffin is positioned in the middle of the aisle, to the side there's a photo of Elvis. His head thrown back in laughter which brings a small smile through my tears. That's how I want to remember him. Full of laughter and love. Instead all I see is the gaping bullet wound in his head. His eyes lifeless and Teresa's screams accompanying the memory.

Sue and Teresa are in the first pew. Angel and Prez to either side of them. Sue's quietly sobbing while Teresa keeps muttering no. Repeating it over and over. She twists the handkerchief in her hand the whole time. I have a feeling that if she stops she will crumble. I wish I was sitting with her, so we could share our pain but I don't deserve her forgiveness. I stay here, out of sight.

Music starts to flow through the church, my heart breaking even more when I hear the song. *The Wonder of You*, Elvis's song, the one he serenaded us all with at any opportunity. Even some of the tough looking bikers look red eyed hearing this.

The service passes by in a teary blur. I only realize it's over when people start heading out of the door. Diane moves over to me. Her own face tear strewn.

She reaches out for my arm. "Come on sweetie, let's get you out of here." At first I think she's showing me sympathy. Then I realize she's just trying to get me out of the away before Sue and Teresa see me. I let her lead me outside.

The graveside service is somber. Teresa collapses as the coffin is lowered into the ground, howling with grief. "Don't leave me Daddy.", Prez tries to lift her to her feet, but she won't move. "You promised me, you fucking promised me you wouldn't leave me Daddy."

Her pain makes my tears flow faster. The guys each say their farewell to Elvis before heading back to their bikes. Teresa hasn't moved. Prez reaches down and lifts her into his arms with such tenderness, carrying her back to the car. My tears haven't stopped at all since I woke this morning.

When they have gone I'm left standing at the graveside, alone. I walk closer, grabbing a fistful of dirt and throw it on the coffin. "I'm so sorry Elvis. I wish it was me lying there instead of you. You didn't deserve this. I love you." Completely broken I head back to the last of the waiting cars.

Chapter Twelve

Eve

When I get back to the clubhouse the wake for Elvis is in full swing. There are bikers and old ladies everywhere, kids too so the club whores have been told to stay away. This is a family affair after all.

I see everyone is deep in conversation with someone else, and has a drink in hand. There's no sign of Teresa, Diane or Sue anywhere. I slowly walk up to the bar, ordering a vodka shot from the prospect on duty. Immediately I ask for another along with a beer, he gives me a worried look but pours the drinks anyway. I don't even like beer but fuck it.

I look around from my lonely perch at the bar. There's rock music playing in the background, and everyone seems to be getting along; they don't even notice me. I don't belong here, I feel so out of place. Ordering another beer to go, I walk back to my room, avoiding everyone on my way.

Stripping out of my black knee length dress, I slip into something a little more comfortable, a tiny vest and sleep short combo. I finish the rest of my beer, then reach for the other bottle. Getting comfortable on the bed, there's a murmur from everyone else having a good time talking about Elvis. I lay on my own, only my thoughts of Elvis to keep me company. I laugh out loud at some of the funny moments, like when he took me and Teresa to a park. There was a huge slide, the thing was so high we were scared to go on, Elvis tried to reassure us it was fine. We didn't believe him so in the end he got up the ladder and went down himself. Now Elvis has always been a big man so halfway down he got stuck and like any normal ten year olds we almost peed ourselves from laughing. The memory still makes me giggle.

About an hour later the music turns louder and I start to become sleepy. Crying all day does that.

***

There's silence when I wake up. Looking over at the clock it's 4:00am. Rolling over I try to get back to sleep but I just can't. Every time I shut my eyes I see either Lola lying butchered on the ground, or my sweet Elvis lying dead. Deciding to give up on sleep I slip on my shoes, making my way to the TV room through the bar. There's no sign of anyone anywhere, they must all be sleeping. I decide to not give a shit, making myself at home behind the bar. After another beer goes down a treat I grab the bottle of Vodka and walk toward the TV room. I feel more comfortable in there, it feels cleaner. It probably isn't but there you go.

While I'm sitting nursing my guilt I see Mutt appear. He probably stayed out of the way earlier with it being so busy. Mutt is the club's dog. They kind of adopted him, well the old ladies did. They'd spotted him outside eating some scraps after a barbecue a few months ago and started to leave food out for him. He's been here ever since. He's kind of scraggy looking, his fur's a dirty gold color, but he's sweet and wouldn't hurt a fly, as long as you don't put him in danger or hurt someone he cares about I guess. Kind of like the members of the club, some of them are scraggy looking, some scary looking, while others are sexy as hell.

I absentmindedly stroke Mutt's fur, swigging from the bottle, wincing as the vodka hits my throat. This is all my fucking fault. Everyone thinks so, I can tell by the way they look at me. Even Teresa thinks this is all down to me and I totally agree. It's my fault her dad was killed. Sue's right, if I hadn't come here he would still be alive. I feel home sick and I desperately want to see my baby girl. The tears are falling freely and I don't bother to stop them. Mutt whines at my feet, I fuss him a little more to let him know I'm fine but it's a lie. I can't do this anymore. I don't belong here. I should go. Satan won't bother me at home will he?

"You shouldn't be drinking by yourself." I jump at his voice. I slowly look up, seeing Angel frowning down at me. He takes the bottle from my hand, shaking his head. "Especially not Vodka."

"So what? Nobody gives a fuck."

Angel sits down next to me. "Why do you say that Princess?"

"Because it's true." My voice is slightly slurred, I really hope he doesn't notice. "Everyone here wants me gone."

"They don't." He really does sound genuine.

I laugh a little. "Of course they do. Even my best friend doesn't want me here anymore and I can't blame her." I take a deep breath to gather myself. "It's all my fault, Angel. He's dead because of me."

I break down into a sobbing mess. Angel reaches over and holds me while I fall apart, bless him. His body is a little stiff, I can sense his awkwardness. I bet he's never had a girl break down in front of him before. The tears continue to come, but I feel better as he holds me. This is what I needed. I just needed somebody to hold me while I cried. I needed someone to talk to, to comfort me.

When I have calmed down I back away a little, smiling at him as I wipe my face with the back of my hand. "Sorry."

"No it's fine, I always have women crying on me."

I laugh. "Yeah, I bet." He shrugs his shoulders. "I just want to go home."

His face becomes deadly serious. "You can't do that."

"Why not? I don't belong here."

"Who says?"

"I can see it on everyone's faces, they don't want me here."

"They're grieving. They'll get over it. None of this is your fault."

"Yeah well, maybe I'll look at swapping my flight tomorrow. I don't think Teresa even wants me at her wedding anymore."

"It's not safe for you yet." I don't bother answering. "If you go home you'll put your daughter in danger."

I stare at him wide eyed. "What?" I'd never even considered that.

"He's a monster, he won't think twice about it. You have to stay here to keep both of you safe."

I don't hesitate to agree. If staying here keeps Elizabeth safe I have no other choice. No way will I put my baby girl in danger.

I grab the bottle back, taking a big gulp. I don't know how I'm going to get through all this. Angel takes the bottle from me, taking a large shot himself. He doesn't even wince at the burn. He takes it like the man he is, then takes a second. Not moving his eyes away from me. "Can't let you drink by yourself." Fuck, he has the hottest blue eyes.

I smile. "You don't have to."

He moves in a little closer. "I want to."

Ok, the temperature just rose. Angel's looking at me like he wants to devour me. I wouldn't say no if he asked me right now.

Angel asks me about my memories of Elvis. I share some funny ones and happy ones from growing up with him in England. I'm shocked that I don't cry. Yes I feel sadness, but I don't cry. It's certainly an improvement. Perhaps I just needed someone to care about me, just for a moment, to ask how I'm feeling. I'm grateful it was Angel. He seems to really listen to what I'm saying, it's a nice change from what I've become used to.

Conversation spirals and we start laughing. It's easy and Angel seems like a good guy. Under the alpha biker image seems to be a normal guy who just likes to be in control. What's wrong with a man who goes after what he wants? I find that incredibly sexy.

"So, why the name Angel?" I finally ask. Whenever I've had chance to speak to a club member I've wanted to know the reason behind there biker names. Last week I asked Disney how he got his. Me being an idiot thought he may have liked Disney films, but boy was I wrong. He laughed at me and told me it's because he loves to watch porn. It's a twisted spin because there's nothing Disney about that. He got that right and I blushed to my roots.

"It's because of my name."

That's all I get. "Which is?"

He sighs. "Gabriel, but I shorten it to Gabe."

Makes sense and it's not crude like Disney's. "I like it." That gets me a killer smile in return.

He suddenly stands, holding out his hand. "Come on, better get you back to bed."

I look at the time and see it's 6:00am. Wow I hadn't realised I'd been out here that long. I let Angel pull me up. He has to help me walk to my room. I'm laughing at myself as we walk because I hadn't realised how much I've had to drink and I keep tripping and stumbling. So not attractive Eve.

When we reach my door, Angel pushes it open, guiding me over to sit me on the bed. "I'll see you tomorrow."

He's turning to leave when I call out to him. He stops in the door way. "Why don't you stay?" He looks unsure so I stand up and walk towards him. "Please?" I whine.

I am so drunk it's fucking embarrassing. Angel reaches up, softly brushing my cheek, just like he did earlier. His eyes burn into me. "You're so fucking cute." He gives me that killer smile and I'm not ashamed to say my panties become wet.

I don't expect it, but it happens. Angel leans in, capturing my mouth with his. His kiss feels amazing and I whimper against him. He wraps his other arm around me, pulling me closer. I feel the long, hard steel length of him. Oh my! He growls against my mouth as he controls me. His tongue dances with mine, making me imagine the wonderful things he could do with it. His soft lips have mine surrendering, but it's all over too soon. He suddenly pulls away from me. I almost fall forward, but he catches me. He stares at me, loudly cursing. "Fuck!" And then he's gone. Storming off out of sight.

Fuck indeed!

Chapter Thirteen

Eve

I wake the next morning feeling out of sorts. I don't know how to feel to be honest. I'm still down from the death of Elvis, I'm going to feel his loss for a long time. I also feel weird because of what happened last night with Angel, maybe I should ask Prez if I can change rooms. It's probably not a bad idea. I don't know why I'm in Angel's room anyway. He obviously doesn't like me. I thought we were getting on great as friends last night but the attraction obviously isn't mutual. He wouldn't have run off like that if it was. How can I not be attracted to Angel? He's fucking gorgeous, rocking a hot body that would make any woman fall to her knees.

When I dress and emerge from my room I'm glad that I can't see him anywhere. I don't think I could handle seeing his face right now. I'm feeling a little undesired. God I'm suffering such a wide variety of emotions right now I don't know whether I'm coming or going.

I'm uncomfortable as well. Not in my surroundings, or what I'm wearing. No. I'm feeling uncomfortable because Angel worked me up and then stopped. You could say I'm sexually frustrated. I need to get laid! I haven't had sex since the night before douche-bag left me. Yeah, he actually did that to me, he knew he was leaving the next day so thought he would get one last shag before he left. Fucking arsehole. He didn't even make me come, but then he never had during our sex life. At the beginning I thought it was just because I was new to it all, but I soon realized that wasn't it. He was just too selfish to worry about my needs. The last few years I'd waited until he fell asleep before pleasuring myself to climax, or sometimes killed two birds with one stone while I was in the shower.

I enter the TV room, instantly spotting Ink. I smile at him, as I move to sit on one of the free sofas. He joins me as soon as my butt hits the cushion. I love Ink, he's funny and likes to flirt a lot. There's absolutely nothing wrong with a little flirting. Plus he's bloody gorgeous. What's the harm in flirting with a hot man?

"How you doing babe?" He smiles over at me.

"I'm OK." Well, that sounded convincing, not.

"Haven't seen you today."

It's 12:00pm. I was too tired after my early morning drinking session and then I was too embarrassed to come out my room and bump into Angel. "I was up late last night."

He nods his head. "Yeah, yesterday was tough."

We both smile sadly and nod. There's nothing I really want to say about yesterday. Not only was it the funeral of the only father I knew, but I felt I'd had no-one to lean on. Until I saw Angel that is.

"So when am I getting my hands on that sweet virgin skin of yours?" Ink wiggles his eyebrows suggestively, and just like that, I'm smiling again.

Ink keeps badgering me to have a tattoo. I've told him before that I haven't got one yet. His reference to virgin skin makes me blush.

"I don't know."

"Aww come on, show me some skin." Ink makes me laugh and it feels so good.

"You're so funny."

He smiles, dimples appearing on his face that make me swoon.

"There is one tattoo, but I don't know." There's a design I've liked for a long time. I think I could trust Ink, he does all the clubhouse art, but I've still not quite convinced myself.

"Just promise you'll come to me when you finally decide to have one done." He gives me his puppy dog eyes.

"I promise." I say laughing.

"Good, because I would hate to kick that sweet ass of yours if I found out you went to someone else."

I can't stop laughing as he continues to tease me. Ink is becoming a real good friend. Looks like for now he's my only friend.

***

Gabe

I had to go on a run with Dragon and Kid this morning. Eve's been on my God damn mind all fucking day. It's messed up all my shit.

Last night I'd gotten up to grab a drink after waking up sweating from yet another fucked up dream. When I saw Eve sitting there on her own with Mutt by her side I felt bad for her. She was obviously feeling a lot of pain for Elvis, and Teresa was so into her own shit that she couldn't see how badly she was hurting her oldest friend.

I sat with her and surprisingly had a good time. Who knew she was so funny, and she's as cute as fuck. Shit I don't think I've ever thought of anything as cute, not even Beth.

When I kissed her I couldn't help myself. She was standing there in front of me, swaying slightly from the drinks she'd had, looking fucking adorable. There I go again. Adorable? Fucking hell.

When I got my shit together I had to pull away. I knew I couldn't stop at a kiss and she was drunk as shit. I had to walk away to stop myself. I don't usually give a fuck if the girls drunk or not. As long as they're up for it I am too, but not Eve. If I'm going to have sex with her I want her completely sober.

Walking into the clubhouse, I'm glad to be back. I was on edge the whole time we were away, worried Satan would strike. I don't know if that was worry for the whole club, or one person in particular.

I scan the bar before walking into the TV room. There she is, sitting on the sofa looking beautiful but she's not alone. She's sitting close to Ink, always that fucker. They're laughing, and Eve's smiling widely and throwing her head back. She looks fucking gorgeous like that. I suddenly see red.

Laughter sounds behind me and I glare over at Dragon. He's been digging at me every opportunity about Eve. Seeing me pissed that she's with Ink, yet again, is funny as shit to this mother fucker.

**

Eve

I feel Angel's eyes on me and tense up. I glance up from Ink's teasing face to see Angel looking over at me. He doesn't look very happy. Oh God I knew it would be like this. I knew it would just be plain awkward. What does he look so pissed at me for anyway? He's the one who leaned in to kiss me, not that I wasn't thinking of doing it, and he pulled back. Not me.

Ink looks over his shoulder to see what caused my laughter to halt. Angel's frown deepens further. Ink looks back at me, he's smiling.

"What's going on here then?"

I innocently shrug. "Nothing."

He gives me a look that tells me he's not buying it. "There's gotta be a reason why he looks like he wants to kill me."

I groan and Ink leans forward. "Tell me babe."

I fill him in on everything that went on last night. The drinking, the embarrassment, and then the kiss. He stays silent once I've finished. "Oh. That's it?"

I slowly nod and he laughs.

"Who would've thought? Angel stopping at a kiss." I must have a dumb look on my face because he continues. "Angel is known for his love of women around here."

Well it's not surprising. He's fucking hot. I've seen the way all the women look at him, fuck I even look at him like that. He would be stupid not to take advantage. Even though it does hurt to find out you're crushing on a womanizer.

Crushing? How fucking old am I?

"Look, I like you babe. Just be careful around him yeah?"

I bite my lip. What the fuck am I doing?

Ink slides closer to me, putting his arm around the back of the sofa. Pulling me in close. "Now you need someone like me babe." He grins at me, those darn eyebrows wiggling again. "If that had been me last night I wouldn't have just kissed you. You're a sexy woman Eve. I would have held you all night and woken up next to you. I would treat you like a queen every day babe."

I feel my face burn red and laugh to shake off the tension. I look up at Angel and see he's sitting at a table, still looking over at us. A few club whores trying to get his attention.

"I better get to bed. I was up late last night."

Ink stands when I do and starts walking back with me. "I'm fine. See you tomorrow."

He nods his head and thankfully leaves me to it.

I enter my room, more frustrated now than when I first got up. Angel left me high and dry this morning and now Ink's words have stoked the fire.

I look down at my bag, peeking out from under the bed, a rush traveling through me. My body heats up and only one thing will put out this fire. Seeing as a certain man isn't here to help me out, the toy in my bag will do the job instead.

I don't know what made me bring it with me, but I'm glad I did now.

***

Gabe

I watch Eve walk off, finishing my beer as quickly as possible. I need to go and apologize to her for fucking up last night.

Ink starts to walk over. "Give us a minute yeah girls?"

The girls walk off without another word. They know how to stay on the good side of club members around here.

"What is it Ink?"

He sits down opposite me, scowling. "Eve's a good girl. I don't wanna see you hurt her."

"What the fuck has it got to do with you?" I seethe.

"I like her."

I stand, forgetting all about my beer. "Don't fuck about in my shit Ink. Only warning you get."

Leaving Ink sitting by himself, I make my way to my room. I fucking miss my room.

As I get closer to the door I think about knocking. I probably should but if she knows it's me I've a feeling she won't open the door and I have to say sorry. I fucked up last night. Seeing her with Ink again made me want to fucking knock him out. I have these feelings that I'm hiding but I don't know what to fucking do with them.

I reach for the door. Fuck it. Quickly yanking the door open I freeze when I see Eve on the bed. Her legs are spread wide, showing me everything and fuck me she's sexy as fuck. Her hands are gripping a purple fucking dildo and as I walk in she's mid thrust, her head thrown back in pleasure and making those sexy fucking moans women make that make your cock throb.

Her head snaps up and she gasps, jumping to hide under the covers. "Angel! What the fuck? Get out."

But I don't. I smile down at her while she flushes in embarrassment. I should go, it would be the right thing to do, but I would regret leaving her when she looks this fucking hot.

"What are you staring at? I said fuck off." She's pissed and embarrassed, her face flushed.

I take a step closer. I love hearing her curse, something about hearing a good girl talk dirty turns me on. "I came to say sorry." Surprise overtakes her face. "I'm sorry for this morning. I acted like a dick."

Her face softens a little. "It's ok."

I shrug my shoulders, hiding my grin. Eve raises her eyebrows. "Sooo, you can go now."

I laugh. "Nah I think I'll stay." Her eyes widen and she grips the sheets tighter.

"Erm, Angel." She glances down at the sheet covering her naked body and I laugh again.

"Don't be embarrassed Princess." I reach over, tucking her hair behind her ear. "You look hot as fuck."

Her breathing becomes faster. I can see her hardened nipples under the sheet. My dick is rock hard right now.

"Fuck, I can't hold back anymore."

***

Eve

As soon as Angel utters the words he grabs the back of my head, capturing me in another steamy kiss. Except this time he doesn't hold back, he means business. I whimper against him as he rips the sheets away from me.

His eyes devour me and my arousal increases. "Fuck baby, you're so sexy."

God I need him right now. He takes the vibrator from me, tossing it aside. "You won't be needing this anymore" he smirks.

He leans down and lies over me, trapping me under his muscled body. His rough clothes graze my naked skin. My hands clutch his leather cut and he shrugs it off. I reach for the hem of his black shirt as he thrusts against me. I feel the need to hold onto him. He quickly jumps up from the bed and strips. He stands before me, proudly stroking his large, thick cock. Fuck me that has to be sexiest thing I've ever seen. I bite my bottom lip. I want him.

I crawl to the edge of the bed and he senses what I want. Stepping closer, still holding his hard cock he comes level with my greedy mouth. I lick the swollen tip, causing him to release a groan. The sound spurring me on, I take him as deep into my throat as I can without gagging. He thrusts his hips as my head bobs and I get drunk on his taste. I suck him hard, his foreskin going back and forth with my mouth and he hisses. Never in my life have I enjoyed giving a blow job as much as this. I reach back, grabbing his tight butt cheeks, bringing his cock deeper into my throat. I gag and he moans in pleasure. "Yeah baby. Gag on my dick. Shove it in."

My eyes water as I gag again and he pulls my mouth from him with a pop. "Lay down Princess."

I do as he says, and before my back hits the mattress I feel his tongue licking my wet slit. I gasp loudly and he wastes no time diving in. He's like a starving man. My legs wrap around his shoulders as I drown in the sensation. I've always wondered what this would feel like but never dreamed it would be this good although I've a feeling Angel is in a league of his own. I was right about that tongue of his. He has pure talent. He bites down on my clit and I scream my release. As soon as I do he spins me over so that I'm now on my front, pulling my legs to position me on all fours. Before I can gather my senses he enters me in one smooth motion. I throw my head back in ecstasy. I have never felt this full.

"Hold on." He grunts before pounding me. I gasp, the feeling of Angel's cock inside of me is incredible. Oh God this is amazing.

I'm screaming so loudly I think the whole clubhouse can hear, but at this moment in time I don't fucking care. I just want Angel to keep pumping his large cock in me. If he stops now I think I will kill him. My boobs are jiggling like crazy as he pumps faster and faster and I start to feel it. No way! Me climaxing from Angels mouth was surprise enough because that's never happened to me but a second orgasm? And during sex? Never happened.

"More." I scream and Angel pumps faster.

"Harder." I demand and he pounds a little harder.

It's not enough so I start to push back on him. Fuck me I'm going to come. Angel reaches down and flicks my clit. All it takes is that one touch and I'm flying into unbelievable bliss. I feel Angel's release and scream, my face planting on the bed.

Angel collapses on top of me and rolls us so he's lying behind me, spooning me. Our breathing matches as we pant together.

"Oh God I'm so hot." I'm sweating like a bitch.

Angel bites my shoulder. "Yeah you fucking are. You dirty bitch."

I can't help but laugh. "Who would have thought sweet little Eve likes it rough?" he murmurs.

"You learn something new every day." I tease.

I jump up from the bed in need of a cool shower. I'm too hot and bothered and need to cool down.

"Where the fuck you going?"

"Shower."

I'm only in there for about two minutes when Angel joins me and I smile. I knew he wouldn't be able to resist. He quickly turns me so that my back hits the cold tile wall, lifting me with ease, I throw my legs around his waist. "Ready for round two?"

I don't have chance to answer before he thrusts into me again. I groan loudly as he fills me, it feels so damned good. Angel continues to slam into me while the water flows over us. His bright blue eyes looking deep into mine as he consumes me. Man this biker can fuck! Just looking at him you know this is a man who will fuck you senseless. That is what he is doing to me right now. I can't think of anything else but Angel as he takes me up against the shower wall. I feel his cock bumping against my cervix, a slight pain that adds to the stunning pleasure. He growls as I scream.

"Scream louder baby." And I do. Every time his thick, luscious cock enters me.

We both scream out our releases and Angel slides me back down the wall. He kisses me, holding my hand as we walk out of the shower. I didn't expect him to be sweet like this, he even grabs the towel and dries me. Well, I think he's sweet until I realize he's just doing it to cop a feel of my body. This makes me laugh and he grins at me. It's a lazy, sexy seductive smile that promises sex with a hint of danger.

We lay down together in his bed. This is all so unreal.

"I don't usually share my bed Princess." His voice is thick with sleepiness, it's so fucking hot.

"Well you can leave." I offer, hoping like fuck he turns me down.

He chuckles. "Nope, not going anywhere." He lays one of his strong legs over mine and an arm over my waist. "And neither are you."

My eyes become heavy as the heat from his body soothes me to sleep.

Chapter Fourteen

Gabe

I wake up with Eve in my arms and I'm surprised I don't feel panicked. There's a little there under the surface because I don't know what this means, but I don't feel like running away from her again.

Thinking back to last night, seeing her with Ink hurt, and I don't know if it's anger or jealousy. I think I need to have a chat with my brother, he says he likes her and I can see he cares for her. Something's happening here, fuck if I know what it is but I will not let anyone stop it. Ink needs to know to step back.

Eve shuffles causing my dick to harden against her back. Last night was totally unexpected. I'd never have guessed there was such a dirty girl hiding under her sweet exterior. I definitely want to experience that again. Tonight if I'm lucky. I just have to make sure I don't piss her off again.

Maybe I should let her come to me this time? I don't want her to make a mistake because she's grieving and no-one else is giving her the time of day. She might not have given up the goods as fast otherwise. I'm a little pissed at the old ladies actually. The only other person talking to her is Ink and he's pissing me off. I hate the idea of him working his way in and getting closer to her than I am. Maybe I should claim her? Somehow I don't think she would like that, but at least my brothers would know to stay away while I work out what the fuck is going on between us. I could do it without her knowing, but she's bound to find out and that would just fuck everything up. She's going home after the wedding so perhaps she just wants a little fun. I can do that, show her what a real man can offer a woman. Ruin her so she'll always compare other men to me.

I look at the time and see I have to get up. I'm meeting Dragon, we're going to see this cop contact of his. The club trusts Dragon's loyalty, but it won't hurt for the President and VP of Severed to be involved.

I don't want Eve waking up to find me gone, but I don't want to wake her. She looks fucking gorgeous sleeping. There's no sadness covering her beauty. Ironically she looks like a sleeping angel. It's the first time since she got here I've seen her look at peace. I do have to leave now though so I quietly get up and dress, she doesn't stir at all so I decide to leave her sleeping as I slip out the door.

***

Eve

When I wake up the next morning I'm beautifully sore, smiling at the memories. Last night was the best sex I have had hands down. I don't even have to think about it. The only competition Angel had was fucking douche-bag and he doesn't even rate a comparison. How am I supposed to move on after sex like that?

The truth is I don't want to, but I can't tell him that. I'm not fucking stupid.

I shift a little, realizing Angel isn't in bed. Maybe he's in the bathroom? Slowly turning over I can see the bathroom door is open. I listen for any noise indicating he's in there, but nothing. I sit up, eyes scanning the room, his clothes have gone. The fucking dick has fucked me and left.

How dare he treat me like one of his club whores.

I get up and shower again, trying to ignore the hot sex flashbacks whilst I wash my hair. I decide to dress in my short denim skirt and tight white vest top, making sure to put on the push up bra that makes the most of my boobs. I'll make him regret treating me like this. He's not getting inside my panties again.

***

After getting some breakfast and soothing my anger a little, Ink approaches me. Perfect. I'm sitting at the bar getting to know the Prospects a little better when he comes over and gives them a nod. I realize this is a signal for them to leave as they give me a smile, leaving me alone with him.

"How did it go last night?" Ink smirks.

My eyes widen and my cheeks become hot. "What do you mean?"

One of his eyebrows lifts. "I saw Angel go to your room last night and I didn't see him for the rest of the night."

Oh. My. God. My face is on fire. Ink laughs, but it doesn't sound sincere. "Chill babe."

I take a big gulp of my water, wishing now that I'd taken up the offer of something stronger.

After a couple of minutes of awkward silence I can feel Ink's eyes on me, I look everywhere but at him.

"You look smoking today Eve."

I give him a smile pushing out my chest, he's back to his flirting. "Thank you."

He strokes a finger down one of my bare legs. "So about this tattoo you want?"

I chuckle. He's not going to give up and I'm coming around to the idea. "It's a heart with wings either side. Some red roses underneath and I don't know whether to have something for my daughter next to it."

He looks like he's picturing my tattoo in his head. "You could have her initials? Either on top or inside?" Yeah that could look good. "Where do you want it?"

I shrug my shoulders. "I don't know."

He looks me over and I know he's checking me out. "I think lower back."

"Lower back it is." I smile widely.

"Why haven't you already had it done?"

I'd told him a little about my douche-bag ex last night. "My ex wouldn't let me."

"He sounds like a great man." Ink frowns and I scoff.

"Yeah you bet."

"Why did you break up?"

"He left me."

"What the fuck?"

"Yep. He'd gone before I woke up and left me a note. He said he didn't want anything to do with either me or my daughter. Said he never even wanted to be a father." I feel some tears building but they're not for him. They're for my baby girl.

Ink strokes my back, soothing me. "Don't get upset over that fucker babe."

"No I'm not. I'm just upset for my daughter."

"How old is she?"

"Two." I grin widely, picturing Elizabeth.

He smiles back. "I bet she looks just like you."

I get out my phone and show him a few pictures of her. Fresh tears gather. I miss her so much.

"She's beautiful Eve." He looks me straight in the eye. "Promise me you won't settle for a fucker like that again."

I'm nodding my head when I notice Teresa walk in. My eyes follow her as she walks out back. There are always members out there so Prez said it would be okay for me to go out there. I really need to talk to her. It's killing me having her mad at me. I came here for her, and now I don't know what to do.

I shoot up from my stool and go after her. Ink grabs onto my arm and I know by the look on his face he's going to tell me to leave her, but I can't. "I need to talk to her."

Ink doesn't look happy but he lets me go. I can sense him following me as I speed walk after Teresa.

She's walking towards a spare bench and I feel eyes on me as I walk closer. They know what I know. She's not going to listen and she's well known for throwing a bitch fit or two, so she's bound to throw one now. I call after her. "Teresa."

She stops walking and turns slowly, a scowl set in place. "I don't wanna talk to you Eve." She dismisses me.

"Please Teresa. I'm so sorry." A tear falls down my cheek.

"I don't have time for this shit right now. Just fuck off yeah?"

That hits me hard. How dare she talk to me like that. I've had enough of people walking all over me. First I took shit from my mother, then douche-bag for years, Angel this morning and now Teresa. The girl I thought was my best friend, my sister. "I lost him too you know." I shout and see her tense. "He was like a father to me and I lost him too. I know it's all on me and I'm so fucking sorry, but I'm fucking hurting too. I've let you talk to me like shit and ignore me but I've had enough. I came here for you. Look what's happened to me now. I'm being hunted by a fucking madman called Satan for fucks sake!"

She takes a step towards me and I stand my ground. "You think that's my fault?" She sneers.

"I didn't say that. I'm saying that you're so hung up in your own shit you can't see I'm hurting as well. You've got everyone here for you and I have no-one. I'm tired of everyone looking at me like I'm shit. Maybe I should just leave and go home."

She gives me a nasty smile, she looks like a total bitch right now. "Yeah, maybe you should. Go on Eve, fuck off home."

I gasp. I don't think about what happens next, it just happens. I lunge forward, pushing her to the ground. She curses at me and jumps up going to grab for my hair. I duck and manage to slap her. Shit, that stings. She lands a punch to my stomach when we're suddenly ripped apart. Each of us still trying to get a last shot in.

The roar of Prez' voice makes us both freeze. "What the fuck?" I sag against the man behind me. Catching his scent I roll my eyes. Fucking Angel. "I thought you were fucking best friends?"

Teresa and I both laugh. "Yeah that was before." she hisses.

"I said I was sorry." I shout.

"Enough! Elvis' death isn't on Eve. Stop this shit now." Angel roars behind me.

Prez turns Teresa in his arms, looking down at her. "He's right sugar."

Teresa breaks down in his arms and he carries her back inside. I look around to see Ink standing close by and around twenty other members stood watching me, including some of the old ladies. They are looking at me differently. Can I hope that that's respect I finally see in their eyes?

Ink steps up to me, I'm still held in Angel's stupidly big sexy arms. He reaches his hand out and I lift mine to meet it, but Angel yanks me back. Bikers and old ladies are watching curiously.

"Come on babe, I'll take you inside." Ink says.

"Nah, I'll do that brother." Angel flips me to face him. His eyes travel over me, inspecting for damage I guess. "You good?"

I nod my head. Angel grips me harder, then throws me over his shoulder in a fireman's lift. I squeal. "Angel! Put me down."

I feel his hand on my backside, ensuring no-one can see up my skirt. "Catch you later Ink."

He carries me past everyone, still flipped over his shoulder. What the fuck is he doing? I look up and see Ink watching us, then lay my head back down in defeat. I don't want to see who we pass, this is embarrassing.

When we get to my room he drops me on the bed. I let out a huff. "I can walk Angel."

"Yeah, but I wanted to carry you." He gives me that sexy ass grin of his.

I frown at him, indicating the door behind him. "You can leave now."

He stuffs his hands in his pockets. "What the fuck? Why you pissed?"

Is he stupid? "Oh let me think? Oh yeah. Might be something to do with me waking up alone this morning, no fucking note or anything."

A lopsided grin appears on his sexy face. "I don't do notes Princess."

I huff, crossing my arms over my chest. His eyes zero in on my boobs. Yeah that's right, have a good look at what you can't have.

"You could have woken me. You made me feel like a whore. Is that what I am Angel? A whore? Well I won't be one."

He frowns down at me and then sits in front of me. "Let's get one thing straight. You ain't a whore and I've never thought you were."

I don't know what to say so I keep my mouth shut.

"I left because I had shit to do with Prez and Dragon. I didn't wanna wake you. You were lying there all peaceful and shit."

Well fuck. I didn't expect him to say that. I feel like an idiot. He could have at least let me know though. What's a girl supposed to think? Hearing that he didn't want to wake me I'm left confused as to how I feel about him.

He sighs heavily and stands. I don't look up at him though. I hear him taking off his boots. "Look at me Princess."

I don't and his hands come to my face, forcing me look at him. He stands back again, slowly unbuttoning his jeans.

"Watch me Eve." He strips before me, I couldn't look away if I wanted to. Angel naked is an image I want to always remember.

He reaches for me, lifting me up. I don't stop him when he starts to undress me. When we're both naked he leads me to the shower.

"Come on, I need to wash off."

I rush to join him. He hands me his shower gel and I immediately get to work. Washing his fantastic body, I show a certain hard part of him a little extra care. When I'm done he returns the favor. His large hands on me feel amazing. I wish every shower could be like this. He turns off the water, stepping out. He picks me up, moving us back to the bedroom, and I start to become even more excited. I'm already worked up from seeing Angel naked and now, more than anything else, I want him to fuck me.

Instead of flipping me like last night, he lays me on my back, settling himself over me. Before his lips can distract me I remind him. "Angel, we need protection. We didn't use any yesterday."

I remembered that shortly after I woke up this morning, realizing how fucking stupid we'd been. He smirks down at me.

"You on the pill?" I nod my head. "I'm clean, I trust you. I don't want anything in between us. It feels too fucking good."

Without waiting for me to answer he enters me and I throw my head back. "Ahhh." I moan loudly.

"Feel me." Angel grunts.

I do. Fuck I can feel him. He begins moving faster and harder, just how I want it. My groans become louder as he hits my sweet spot.

"That's it, scream for me. You like it hard Princess?"

"YES." I scream. Angel pounds into me harder and harder with each thrust.

"Angel I'm going to come." I whimper. He flicks my clit and I shatter into a million pieces. I'm grasping his back, digging my nails in, as I fall.

Angel hasn't finished with me yet, slamming his mouth on mine, continuing to thrust into me. My eyes close, I'm sure they're crossed, my orgasm feels that fucking good.

Angel lifts my legs higher, resting them on his strong shoulders. I moan loudly again as he fills me even deeper. He's growling my name and I greedily take what he's giving me. He's slamming into me so hard that it's not long before I feel the burn inside again. It's strong and I don't know if I want to let it release.

"Give it to me." Angel growls, I try my best to hold on.

Angel slams into me harder, lifting my bottom just a little bit higher, deepening the sensation so much more. I scream my release and feel Angel follow straight after.

We lay quietly together as we come down. Once I have my breath back I get up to go and clean myself. When I get back to the bedroom Angel is already half dressed. I'm so tired right now but start to get dressed again. Angel stops me. "You get into bed, I've got some shit to sort out."

I don't know what to say. Is this good or bad?

He throws me his shirt, watching me as I pull it over my head. Looking over at me he smiles. His shirt is huge on me, coming level with my knees.

"I don't need that right now."

He turns to put on his cut and I gasp. There are long red gouges down his back. Did I do that?

He turns, winking at me when he sees I've noticed his back before walking out the door.

I go and sit on the bed in a stunned silence. What the fuck was that?

Chapter Fifteen

Eve

When I wake I'm still confused about what happened last night. Angel had apologized for leaving me the other night then left straight after sex again.

I know to him this thing between us is just casual sex, but for me his leaving seemed a little too casual. I don't know if I can carry on like this. I'm one of those women who puts her emotions into relationships. I know if I carry on sleeping with Angel I'll just get hurt in the long run. I'm not sure I can handle this style of casual hook up.

I dress in my tight skinny jeans and short crop top, showing off my belly button. I usually feel self conscious in this top because it shows a lot of skin, however, after last night I'm in a daring mood. Plus it's hot as fuck today. Pulling my hair into a messy bun and slipping on my Converse, I walk out of my room with my head held high. I will not let Angel bring my mood down like yesterday.

No sooner have I left my room than I see Diane, spotting me she walks straight over. I stand my ground, waiting to hear what she has to say. She gives me a slight smile, standing right in front of me. "Don't worry, I'm only here to say sorry. I heard all that yesterday. I hadn't realized that's how you were feeling." She places a hand on my shoulder and gently squeezes. "Sorry honey."

I smile back. It's nice to have her talking to me again. "Thanks, how are Sue and Teresa doing?"

She pulls a face. "They'll be fine in their own time. Your show impressed all the old ladies around here. You've got to show you can hold your own if you want to find your place in this club. Good on ya girl." This draws a small laugh from me.

I can see Ink across the room standing with Disney and Cowboy. Diane follows the direction of my eyes, just as Ink gives me a smile. She looks back at me, raising her eyebrows. "Ink?"

"What? No, he's a friend." I protest. She gives me a funny look.

"Really."

"OK then, what about Angel? I saw the show you guys put on yesterday remember." I bite my lip and lower my head before she can see me blushing.

"Oh I see." Diane gives a belly laugh. "You've got a thing for our VP."

My head snaps up, my eyes widening. "No I don't."

This makes her laugh again, causing Ink, Dragon and Cowboy to walk over. Dragon wraps his arm around Diane, bringing a smile to her face as Ink and Cowboy stand either side of me.

Cowboy looks at me and winks. "Looking good."

I smile in return before blurting out my question. "So Cowboy, what's the story behind your name?"

He gives me a naughty grin and I just know this is going to be more like Disney's name than Ink's. "Well sugar, I got my name because I like to be ridden cowboy style. Good and hard."

My mouth widens and I hear chuckling around me. I knew it. "If you ever wanna show me how well you can ride sugar, you just let me know."

"Sure." I squeak, causing yet more laugher.

"Babe, is today the day?" I turn to Ink as Diane asks what he's talking about. "She ain't got any ink, I wanna get my hands on that virgin skin of hers."

"Go on girl, what else you got planned for the day?" Diane asks me.

She does have a point. "She even knows what she wants, she's just being a pussy." Ink winks at me.

I glare at him. "I am not."

The look he gives me in return makes me want to stomp my foot like a child, luckily I hold back. "Fine. Let's do it."

His eyes widen. "Now?"

"Yep." Might as well get it done while I'm feeling brave.

Ink grins widely, holding his hand out. "Come on then."

He leads me past the office and game room, stopping at a door on the end. When he opens it up I see it looks just like a tattoo shop inside. So this is where Ink does all his work.

We talk about my tattoo, Ink drawing it out on a piece of paper. It looks amazing. Better than I imagined. There's a black and white heart with angel wings either side, under that there's a small line of realistic looking pink roses, and inside the heart there's a deep red cursive letter E to represent my baby girl and Elvis. I love it!

I decide my lower back is the perfect place to put it. I lay on the bed on my stomach, the nerves starting to creep in. "You'll be fine babe." Ink tries to reassure me.

I laugh a little and he pats my back. "You know what nearly all the women I tattoo say to me?"

"What?"

"That they can handle anything after giving birth."

I scoff. "Yeah well, I'm not very good with pain."

The sound of the needle fills the silence. "You tell me if it's too much and I'll stop."

***

About an hour later I no longer have virgin skin. If Ink had told me it would take this long I think I may have rethought the idea, but I'm glad I finally have my tattoo. The shading in and coloring took a little time and I'd had to stop Ink half way through for a little bit. I'm a wimp what can I say?

"Wow Ink, it looks amazing!" I check out the reflection in the mirror, even with the redness around it I'm so pleased with it.

Right above my backside, where my jeans rest, sits my new tattoo. It looks sexy as hell!

"That's one sexy tat." Ink gloats.

I give Ink a huge grin and he advises me on how to care for it, placing a gauze over it to protect it.

I head back to my room to put on a dress, I want to avoid advertising to all and sundry that I've acquired a new tattoo.

***

Gabe

I'm sitting outside shooting the shit with my club brothers when I see Eve walk out wearing a dress that makes me want to rip it straight off. I'm happy to see she's with Diane and Kid's old lady, Sarah. I heard the old ladies were impressed that she stood up to Teresa yesterday. In this life you have to show you're worth their respect and she did that. Some of the club whores have been gossiping about her too, nasty stuff because they hate the old ladies and they're jealous. Not that Eve is an old lady but they see how she is, Eve's old lady material. She'd be perfect.

I shake those thoughts away when I hear Cowboy laughing with some of the other brothers.

"He's fucking hanging on, brother's desperate for that pussy. Even gave her a tattoo today." The brothers are laughing about someone's latest conquest. These men gossip as much, if not more, than the women.

I realize they're talking about Ink, it must be him if the guy tattooed someone.

"Who you bitching about?" I call over to Cowboy.

He swaggers over, shaking his head. "Fucking Ink, been on the chase again. He finally got her to agree to a tattoo, bet the fucker enjoyed every second."

I lean forward, clenching my jaw. I've got a bad feeling I know who he's talking about, but ask anyway. "Who?"

Cowboy must realize he's dropped his brother in it, but inclines his head over to where Eve is sitting. I'm his VP and rank higher than Ink. "Teresa's friend, Eve. His dick's been hard for her ever since she stepped in here."

What the fuck?

Ink gave Eve a tattoo? I don't fucking like this at all!

Last night I left Eve after the best sex I've ever had to go and find Ink and warn him off, but he'd gone out on a run with some of the brothers. He needs to stay away from her while I figure out what's going on between me and her. I don't know what's happening, but I do know that I don't like Ink sniffing around. Eve's been under me for the last two nights. I'm not fucking sharing her.

Without another word to Cowboy I head over to Eve. She's got her back to me. Diane and Sarah spot me and they can tell from the look on my face I'm not happy about something. They both stand from the bench at my approach, giving their excuses as to why they need to leave.

I stand behind Eve, looking down at her. "Heard you got a tat?"

She quickly turns around, her hand over her heart. "Angel you scared the shit outta me!"

I feel a little guilty. It's starting to get dark out here, she's a little jumpy, with my brother after her so it's understandable. I don't show what I'm feeling, instead I stay standing over her. "I said heard you got a tattoo."

She gives me a weird look, giving me the once over. "News travels fast around here." I nod my head, hands shoved into my jean pockets to keep me from dragging her somewhere private and sinking myself into her sweetness. She huffs loudly. "Yes I got a tattoo, geez is that a crime?"

Fuck she's cute. I hide my smile. "When Ink is after a taste of your pussy, yes."

Eve's mouth drops open and she quickly stands. "Ink is not like that, he's a friend! What's it to you anyway? You don't give a shit!"

"He wants you."

"So what? I'm single, I'll do whatever and whoever the fuck I want."

She goes to step away but I grab her arm. I don't want her leaving pissed at me again. It seems she's always angry with me. Eve looks up at me and I don't know what to say. I can't tell her she's not single because that would mean we're something, yet I don't want her with Ink, or any other man.

She snatches her arm away, marching off. I'm watching her walk away, looking sexy as fuck, when I see Ink walk up to her. Fuck this shit. I follow as quickly as I can. Just as Ink approaches her I grab her, flipping her over my shoulder. She screams out so I give her a smack on the ass. I carry on walking into the clubhouse, most people are in the TV room or outside as I walk past the bar and put her down near the clubs church room.

She slaps my chest when I put her down. "What the fuck do you think you're doing?" I don't answer. "You need to stop doing that. You can't just keep picking me up whenever you feel like it, you're acting like a fucking caveman".

I step closer to stop her ranting. She glares up, her face softening when she sees my smile. "What's going on Angel?"

I lean my forehead on hers, breathing her in. "I don't know."

"You wanna see my tattoo?" She offers coyly.

I lean back, nodding. I want to see how Ink marked her. She bites her lip, looking around. "Maybe we should go back to my room so I can show you."

Eve goes to leave but I push her back against the wall. Where the fuck did he tattoo if she's blushing over showing me? "Where is it?"

"The bottom of my back." She looks embarrassed as she gestures at her dress.

I'm pissed that Ink got to touch her soft skin, but I want to see this tattoo. I turn her around, her back is facing me, slowly pulling up the back of her dress. Eve tries to stop me. "Angel, we can't. Not here."

I lean close into the crook of her neck, between her ear and shoulder and whisper. "Yeah Princess, we can."

I feel her shiver and pull back. Lifting her dress again, my dick hardens when I get to her arse and spy her pink lace underwear. Fuck I love this tiny lacy shit. Fucking turns me on. Eve whimpers slightly. She'll be wet now just from my touch, I love the effect I have on her. She enjoys sex with me as much as I enjoy sex with her. I spot the gauze covering her tattoo, telling her to hold her dress up. Hands free now, I ease the gauze away, standing back to admire her artwork. It's a good looking tattoo, sexy as hell. Forgetting for a moment that Ink put it there I lean forward, kissing just below it, right above her arse. I breathe in a sharp breath, before licking a trail up her smooth back.

Dropping the dress Eve spins around, smiling. "You like it?"

"Princess, you really have to ask?" She leans her head to one side, looking a little unsure. I move into her so she can feel how hard I am. "You feel that? I fucking love it. Now, how 'bout you give me those lips?"

She grins, leaning forward, smacking her mouth against mine. My hands reach under her dress, grabbing her lace covered cheeks. I growl into her mouth, causing Eve to shiver. Her tiny arms wrap around my neck as she tries to get closer. Tightening my grip on her bottom, I lift her and she wraps those long legs of hers around me. Still kissing, I lead her to one of the rooms just past the games room. It's where the old ladies come to escape the men and club whores during the day. It will be empty this time of evening. They'll either be beside or under their old men right now.

Bumping the door open with my back we make our way into the darkness. The old ladies have put up screens in here to partition the walls, creating different rooms in one for all their girly shit.

I smash Eve's back to the wall and grind my hardness against her. I need to be inside her. Now.

I'm about to undo my fly when I hear movement behind one of the screens. On high alert I slowly lower Eve, standing in front of her, pushing her behind me slightly. There's a moan and we slowly walk towards the noise. When I see what's causing the noise I smirk. Dirty bastards. I shake my head, silently laughing, motioning for Eve to come closer, gesturing for her to keep quiet. She tiptoes over, her eyes widening at the sight in front of us. They can't see us, but we can definitely see them.

Eve

When I see what Angel is pointing to my eyes widen and I'm more aroused than when I was caught spying on the foursome. That's probably due to the fact that the foursome was tacky, but this in front of me is between two people I know love each other. Plus I'm standing with Angel, so why wouldn't it be arousing?

Just beyond the screen, I can see Diane bent over a sofa, her arse on show. Behind her is her old man Dragon, both of them completely naked.

Dragon has a long whip, he's holding it high, ready to strike, and I gather myself for what's about to happen.

He brings the whip down quickly with a swoosh, hitting Diane's arse. Her back arches and she lets out a loud moan. I bite my lip, silently watching as Dragon continues to whip her, bringing Diane more pleasure than I thought possible from a whip. Her backside is covered in angry looking red welts. Dragon discards the whip, entering her quickly from behind. My panties are soaked. Dragon is literally fucking her brains out. I can tell when Diane reaches her climax as she shouts his name with her head thrown back in utter bliss. Dragon isn't finished, he slowly lifts her and I see her hands are restrained with cuffs. He lays her on the floor, telling her to leave her hands above her head, or else. If I was Diane I would keep my hands where he told me to. Dragon kisses down her body, only stopping when he gets between her thighs. My legs clamp together as I watch him feast on her, fuck me this is hot to watch. I look at Angel and see he's watching me. I quickly turn away. When I look back Diane has moved her hands and Dragon gives her a spanking with his hand as punishment. From the moans of pleasure coming from her I don't think Diane sees it that way. When Dragon starts to pound into her again Angel grabs my hand, deciding it's time to go.

I agree, reluctantly, I don't want them to catch me watching. That would be embarrassing.

Angel keeps his hand in mine as he marches ahead of me. My legs quicken, trying to keep up with his pace. Everyone seems to be having a good time and drinking as we move through the room, but we don't stop. Angel is on a mission to get me back to my room. I don't argue, I need him right now. Watching Diane and Dragon having raw kinky sex has turned me on so much that I think if Angel even thinks of teasing me, I'll jump his bones.

He loudly slams the door shut behind us and attacks me. We fall to the bed in a frenzy, tongues dance and teeth clash. I can't seem to get close enough to him. He quickly undresses himself and then me. When I feel his warm body against mine I sigh, I love this feeling.

"I knew you were a dirty girl hiding under all that sweetness." Angel growls between kisses. His words make me squirm.

"I need to be in you Princess." He turns me over fast so I'm laid on my stomach. I totally surrender when it comes to Angel. He lifts my hips so they're level with his hard cock. My head resting on the bed, this is something I'd never tried before Angel. Half my body is lifted in the air, supported by Angel. Then he's inside me, it feels so good my eyes almost roll to the back of my head. Angel completely has control, pushing me away from his cock and then pulling me back again. I scream every time he slams me back onto him. He's so deep it's almost too much for me to handle. My hands grip the sheets as I come undone.

"Angel!" I scream and he groans, deep in his chest.

He hasn't finished yet, his assault continues. His hands becoming faster and he's pushing me off then back onto his cock. He begins thrusting, causing him to hit even deeper inside me as we join.

"Oh my God Angel!" I scream again. I can feel it, I'm going to come again.

"Say my name Princess." He growls.

"Angel!" I return, earning another powerful thrust.

"My other name."

It takes me a few minutes to figure out what the hell he's talking about, my mind fogged from this amazing sex. He wants me to call him Gabe? But everyone calls him Angel.

He slams into me, making me scream. "Princess." He warns.

He's close and so am I, so I do what he wants. I scream his name as I'm about to come.

"Gabe! Fuck me Gabe! Fuck me hard!"

And he does. He slams into me with no mercy and we fall onto the bed exhausted and limp.

Chapter Sixteen

Eve

I wake to gentle prodding. Slowly opening my eyes to see Angel looking down at me; I'm pretty sure that's a look of lust in his eyes. "I've got to go Princess, club business."

He leans down, placing a gentle kiss on my forehead. I'm shocked. I never expected that from this hunky, tough biker. I'm not one to complain, so I flash him a grateful smile, not wanting to say anything to ruin it.

I look over to the clock, groaning when I see how ridiculously early it is. We had a late night last night. Filled with hot sex, some rough, some gentle, which really surprised me. Angel had an odd look in his eyes as he thrust inside me, his strong arms surrounding me. That look did something to me, it ignited something deep inside and exploded as I climaxed along with him.

Angel catches my look and laughs at me. "You're the one who complains when I get out of bed and just leave."

I throw a pillow at his back as he puts on his boots. It misses him, falling to the floor. "Cheeky fucking prick."

He quickly turns with a devilish grin. I lay back down, pulling the sheet over my head to hide from him. The sheet's quickly drawn back and I see

Angel's gorgeous face looking down at me. He smoothes my hair from my face. "You really are something." He licks up my neck, turning my anger to passion. "Catch you later Princess."

He stands, shrugging on his cut, all the while still grinning at me. I mutter unintelligible curses as he confidently walks out. Fuck that man is pure sex appeal.

Turning back to the comfort of my remaining pillow, I pull the warm sheets back up. I fall back into a blissful sleep, naked images of a beautiful biker filling my dreams.

***

The next time I wake it's a much more sensible hour. I yawn loudly and stretch. I've decided today is the day. I need to talk to Teresa. I know she's grieving, I can see how hurt she is. I'm still hurting, it's a pain that will be there for some time. As hard as it is, you need to get up and try to act like normal. It's what Elvis would have wanted. He didn't like all this sappy crap, he would want us to get on and live. Teresa is not pushing me away any longer. We've been friends for too long. We should be helping each other right now, leaning on one another instead of her hating and blaming me. Knowing the kind of person she is, I know what she's doing. She's putting the blame on me to give her a channel for her pain, but I've had enough. I'm not taking it any more, I lost Elvis as well.

I quickly dress in my tiny denim shorts and a strappy colored vest, making sure my tattoo is still covered by the gauze. Last night Angel helped me apply cream to it and place a new gauze. I was shocked at the sight of blood on the old one, but Angel assured me it was normal, I'm glad he was there actually, because if I'd seen that alone I would have freaked the fuck out.

I find my Converse under the bed and go in search of my lost friend. Having not found her in the main areas of the clubhouse, I head to the room she shares with Prez.

Knocking on the door I hear a muffled voice from the other side. "Fuck off."

That's Teresa alright. I choose to ignore her and open the door. Walking in like it's completely normal for me.

"I said Fuck off." She says more loudly this time, when she sees me she glares. "And that especially means you."

The venom in her voice is a new addition. I've seen her look of disgust many times on some of our early nights out, when she didn't approve my choice of outfit, or drink. Teresa is a bossy girl who loves to get her own way. Some people call her a bitch, but she's like a sister to me and I love her no matter what.

"Well you'll just have to put up with me 'till I've said my piece then, won't you." I put my hands on my hips, standing my ground this time. "I'm not putting up with your shit any more Tess. For fuck's sake, you're getting married in two days. You're my best friend, I can't take this shit anymore. I want this sorted, because we can't carry on like this."

Teresa looks up at me. She did look angry, until I mentioned her wedding. Then grief shows and she starts sobbing. "I can't get married without my Dad, Eve." She starts to shake now, "I need him, I need my Dad." she wails.

I haven't seen Teresa this broken since we lost her mother. She was completely devastated, but this is something else. Elvis has been her rock for so long and she always was a daddy's girl. When her mum passed it was Elvis who finally brought her out of her sadness and eased her grieving. I'm not sure I can follow in his huge footsteps, but I have to try, for her. I slowly move to the bed, cautious she will shout at me to go away, but she doesn't. I sit myself down beside Teresa and pull her into my arms. I'm shocked and relieved that she lets me help her. Grateful that she lets me hold her while she grieves. This is what it should have been like from the beginning.

After a while her sobbing slows as she becomes exhausted from her tears. She manages to gather herself a little as she looks up at me. "I know it's not your fault Eve, not really. This just hurts so fucking much, I needed to blame someone. You were there and it was easier to put the blame on you."

Knowing Teresa as I do, I know that's as much of an apology as I'm ever going to get.

We spend the next couple of hours sharing our favorite memories of Elvis. The time he grounded us when he caught us sneaking out to a party; the numerous times he found us on the doorstep after partying all night and put us to bed. Even trying to talk to us about the birds and the bees when we were twelve. That memory has us rolling with laughter. It feels so good to share these memories with her. There are so many happy stories surrounding Elvis, that's the way we need to remember him.

When our laughter stops she gives me a sad smile. "Thanks Eve, I really needed this."

"What's happening with the wedding?" I question. Teresa looks at me, her face showing how torn she is.

"Prez wants to go ahead with it, he practically begged me to. God I've been so horrible to him. But I can't do it without him Eve. He was giving me away. I just want to put it off for now."

I'm surprised by the tone of defeat in her voice. She's never been a quitter.

"Elvis wouldn't want that, Sweet. He'd be the first to tell you to 'get your bloody arse down that aisle now darlin'." I use my best Elvis impression, it's so bad Teresa actually cracks a smile.

"Yeah I know he would."

"Who owns you Teresa?" I question. She looks up at me in confusion, but with a little fierceness I recognize as my friend.

"No one fucking owns me." she snaps. That's the Teresa I'm looking for.

"So, if no one owns you, why would you need someone to give you away?" That got her attention. "Go and marry the man you love."

She has tears in her eyes but nods anyway.

We spend the rest of the afternoon simplifying the wedding plans and Diane joins us. I can't look at her, every time I do all I see is her bent over with her arse in the air being whipped by Dragon. I'm trying not to let it show in my face. I'm obviously not successful because Diane turns to me. Looking me over.

"You okay there Eve, you're looking a little flushed."

I burst into giggles. Teresa looks at me, and I can tell she wants me to spill. I do a quick shake of my head, our signal for 'we'll talk about it later', and she gives me a smile of understanding.

Wedding plans all sorted and final. Diane leaves me alone with Teresa, she's barely left the room when Teresa pounces. I've missed this so much that it doesn't take long before she has me repeating everything I saw last night between Diane and Dragon. Teresa is holding her sides laughing.

Apparently Angel and I weren't the first to walk in on them. Teresa tells me they're not shy about being watched. Well that explains why they were there instead of their room then!

We chat a little longer before my stomach starts rumbling, reminding me I've not eaten today. I manage to persuade Teresa to come along with me. People look at us as though we're going to go at each other at any moment. She's not bouncing around with joy, but at least she looks a little happier than she has the last few days. I'm happy to see we seem to have recovered some of our friendship, although it doesn't feel quite the same as it used to. At least it's a start.

***

Gabe

After dealing with our club business, I stopped by the cemetery. Prez and the rest headed back, but Dragon stayed with me. I've been sitting at my mother's grave for an hour or more, trying to understand how this woman could have raised such different sons. For as long as I could remember she'd always brush off Satan's behaviour as "boys will be boys", never grasping the evil he was becoming. Even when Beth died, she refused to accept it was his fault. Always reminding me that Beth had chosen to end her own life. Not wanting to upset her I didn't argue.

She made me promise I wouldn't seek revenge on my brother. The club had ostracized him for his part in the rape, and to her that was punishment enough. I didn't agree but I loved my mother, and no matter how much I wanted to, I couldn't break my vow to her. When he patched in at Carnal he had little to do with our mother. I'm sure that proved too much for her weakened heart. She faded away, not living to see the year end.

I rise slowly. "Sleep well Mama, I'll always love you."

As I'm making my way back to my bike I pause by Elvis' grave. The flowers are still there, but it's too early for the gravestone to have gone up yet. I sense a presence behind me, turning slightly I see it's the priest.

"The bible may quote an eye for an eye Gabriel, but I'm afraid the justice system doesn't quite agree with it."

He's not a stupid man, he's heard what's happening between our two clubs and who's responsible for Elvis death.

"Don't worry Father." I reassure him. "I'm not a bad man."

I pause before adding. "But I'm not a good man either."

***

I'm heading back to my bike, when some punk jumps out of the shadows and starts to wave a fucking knife around like an idiot, advancing on me. For fuck's sake he's hardly old enough to be out of diapers. By the way he's swinging the blade around, he has no idea how to use it, he's made a huge mistake taking me on.

"Where's the fucking girl?" he sneers, thrusting at my gut. The blade scratches against my cut making me pissed. Fuck, if he's marked it he's a dead man. I'm just about to lunge when Dragon sneaks up behind him, grabbing the wrist with the knife and twisting sharply. The sound of breaking bones penetrates the night air. Followed shortly by the punk's childish screams. I shake my head in annoyance. Dragon pulls his now broken wrist up his back, forcing him to the ground on his knees.

"Who the fuck sent you?" Dragon growls.

I can't see a club patch anywhere on the kid, but he looks like he could be a fucking prospect or, an amateur bounty hunter. When he doesn't answer, Dragon twists the broken wrist some more.

"No-one!" He yelps, pain causing his voice to break. God he really has no experience in this shit at all.

"I'm from Carnal but they don't know I'm here. Satan's getting frustrated, taking it out on everyone. I figured I'd find out where the girl was and earn my patch."

Pathetic. Squealing so quickly. He shouldn't have said anything at all. Club rules.

He's whimpering now. This fucker wouldn't make it in our club never mind making it in Carnal MC! He's not tough enough or bright enough for either.

I'm not reassured by the news Satan is getting frustrated though. That means he'll be upping the ante, becoming even more fucking psycho . We've timed our setup plan for the day after Prez's wedding, just three days away. Have we got enough time left?

I need to see Eve. I need to know she's okay, and fuck it I want to sink balls deep into her again. All night long if I can.

I kick the prospect in the balls. He'll be out of action for a while now. Motioning to Dragon we leave him where he's curled up crying, heading back to our bikes and our women.

Chapter Seventeen

Eve

Teresa and I are still laughing and tearfully reminiscing over Elvis and our childhood when Prez walks in. He's followed by several of the members who all spread out between the bar and lounge area. I don't spot Angel anywhere but I notice that when Prez sees Teresa and I sat together he smiles. A lot of tension seems to ease away with that smile, it must have been tough for him to see Teresa falling apart.

"I see you've finally spoken to your girl then." He says to Teresa whilst smiling at me.

Teresa looks up at him, then over at me. "Yeah, we're cool."

He leans down, giving her a deep kiss. "That's good baby."

He tells her he needs her in his room because he's missed her all day. Just before they leave Prez leans into me, wrapping his hand around the back of my head, kissing my forehead. He gives me a wink and a silent thank you before dragging a laughing Teresa back to his room. She's not a hundred percent back to herself, but it's nice to see some of her spark again.

As I'm goofily smiling after them Ink comes to stand by my side. "Hey babe, how's the tat?"

"It's fine. Angel put some cream on it for me last night." His smile falters and I realize I probably shouldn't have said that. Then again, why shouldn't I? Ink and I are friends, I should be able to tell him.

We walk into the bar, sharing a few drinks together and enjoying a bit of harmless banter. That's why we get on so well, we bounce off each other, but other than that there's no spark. Don't get me wrong, Ink is gorgeous but he's not the one who gets my heart pumping. Cowboy and Disney come over to join us and I can't help feeling a little relieved. I don't know why, but I have the feeling Ink sees me as more than a friend. The way his face changed, when I let it slip that Angel helped me soothe my itching tattoo last night was a hint. Now that Cowboy and Disney have joined us, it seems like Ink has returned to being the easy going friend I have come to know. I relax.

"So I see you and queen bitch have made up." Disney jokes.

"Don't call her that and yes we have. Well, we've spoken and cleared the air a little."

"Good, maybe Prez will stop being a dick then."

I giggle. I've come to notice these men like to gossip.

Cowboy downs the rest of his beer, slamming the empty glass down on the bar. "Who's up for a game of pool?"

"I'm in." Disney answers.

Ink turns to me. "How 'bout it babe?"

"I don't know how to play." I haven't been in the pool room since I saw the prospects enjoying Lola, I'm a little uncomfortable about going back there.

Ink takes my drink from me, pulling me along as we follow Cowboy and Disney. "Come on. I'll teach you."

***

Gabe

I'm still feeling a little on edge after bumping into Carnal's prospect and hearing that Satan's getting frustrated. I have this overwhelming need to see Eve and make sure she's safe.

When I see her walking through the bar, her hips swaying, tits and ass bouncing, I want to taste her all over again. I look around at my brothers watching her with a mixture of lust and respect. Yeah Eve is old lady material and she's going to be mine.

Last night I held her after she spoke to her daughter back in England. It was early morning over there so her daughter was wide awake. Eve put her on speaker so I could hear her squeaky high pitched voice. Their conversation was adorable, I could see how much she loved her daughter. She even told her she had a friend called Angel sitting next to her. I said hello, we laughed at the fact her daughter kept repeating my name. When she finished the call Eve began to cry, she misses her daughter so much. We need to sort this shit out so Eve will be safe and can reunite with Elizabeth.

I see her walking by Ink and he has her laughing in seconds, my anger begins to boil. Why does this feel like déjà vu to me?

They're walking out of the bar, possibly towards the game room. I hope he's not giving her another fucking tattoo. I won't allow it. I see red when Ink wraps his arm around her shoulder as he leads her away.

This is not fucking happening. She's been under me for the past three nights, she's as good as claimed so what the fuck is he doing? Hell fucking no!

I follow them, hearing Dragon on my tail. "Need to set him straight brother. Anyone can see you're fucked up in that girl."

I stop and spin on him. "What?"

Dragon gives me a huge grin. "Don't fuck with me Angel. We can all see how you feel about her." He shrugs his shoulders. "Maybe I'm wrong and Ink should claim her."

He carries on walking as I stand still. I don't want that to happen. I'm not going to let it. This shit ends now.

I walk past Dragon, ignoring his chuckles. Yeah my brother fucking got to me and he knows it.

When I enter the games room I stand and watch. She looks as gorgeous as ever, my anger fades a little. She manages to do that to me. She soothes the beast in me that I've always been afraid is a gene I share with my twin.

I watch her as she tries to play against Cowboy and fails. My anger quickly returns and grows when I see Ink come up behind her, showing her how to play. He slowly bends her over, I can see how much he enjoys it, but her face isn't showing the same. She's embarrassed and looks a little awkward. My fists clench as I march over there.

When I reach the table, I pull him away from her. Eve gasps and Ink shouts loudly. "What the fuck?

I slam him against the wall, my hand wrapped around his neck. "Fucking hands off."

"She ain't yours." Ink whines.

My grip on him tightens. I hear a voice shouting my name. I realize it's Eve so I focus on her, she becomes visible as my madness clears. "Angel! Let him go!"

I realize Ink's struggling to breathe so I let him go, he drops to the floor. I look over at Eve. She looks shocked. "What are you doing?"

She looks torn, I know she wants to check on Ink as he coughs on the floor. Eve smartly decides to stay put. Ink slowly stands, glaring over at me. "You haven't claimed her. I've done nothing wrong."

He's partly right. I may not have claimed her, but I've shared a bed with her more than once. She's not a club whore, she's different. "Take this as me claiming her!" I growl.

"You're both fucking insane!" Eve storms out, the brothers giving her a wide berth as she passes.

I land a punch on Ink's jaw, sending him back to the floor. "Stay the fuck away."

I don't look back as I storm after Eve. I can smell her, the scent making my dick jump. I catch sight of her making her way out back. I know Prez said it's safe for her out there, but I still don't like it. Especially when the sun's going down, and I've just heard word from Satan's prospect that he's pissed.

When I run out, I see there are only a handful of men out here. "Get lost." I shout, they slowly move inside, wondering what's wrong with me.

Hearing my voice Eve turns around, the fire in her eyes turning me on. I love it when she gets feisty.

"Come to claim me?" She sneers, her hand on her hip.

"If you're offering." I can't help it, I love it when she bites back.

"I'm getting sick of this shit Angel. I don't think I can handle this anymore."

I'm about to go to her when she glares at me. "You really embarrassed me in there."

"Princess, I've told you before. That man is after you."

She closes her eyes, nodding her head. When she opens her eyes again, she sighs and shocks the shit out of me. "Yeah I know, but I thought we were just friends. That's how I see him anyway, why did I have to go and fuck it all up?"

"No, that's not on you. That's down to him. I can't fucking blame him to be honest."

She cocks her head to the side and my dick hardens. Why the fuck has she got to be all sweet and adorable? I take a step towards her, taking her face in my hands.

"You don't see how fucking beautiful you are." She blushes and looks away. "No look at me Eve." When her eyes are back on me I kiss her soft lips. "The fact you don't know how fucking sexy you are, makes you hot as hell."

She laughs, the sound hitting me right in my gut. This girl's doing crazy shit to me. I never wanted to settle for one woman again, but fuck, Eve has me thinking I might. Shit.

"You're not too bad yourself." She laughs as I pick her up. Her head falls back and I stare up at her. She's so fucking beautiful, I'd hurt any fucker who lays a hand on her.

When she stops laughing she looks down at me. "Angel?"

I slide her back down my body. "Yeah?"

"What did you mean by claiming me?"

I stop. Shit. "Well, in this world when we see a woman we want as our own, we claim them, it's a sign to the other brothers that she's taken."

"And you want to do that with me?"

"Yeah I do, Princess."

She seems to think hard about something, then smiles up at me. "Okay."

A growl erupts deep within my chest. I hold her against me, capturing her mouth with mine. Her arms wrap around my neck and I pick her up, walking back to the clubhouse building. When we reach the brick work in the shadows, I let loose. She does something to me no other woman has ever done. I can feel her need as much as my own. Right now I need to make her come.

Making sure we're on our own I set her down, dragging her shorts down her long slender legs. I'm happy to see she's wearing her usual tiny lacy underwear, black this time. I lean into her, covering her body with mine. I slide my fingers down and into her wetness. Fuck, she's already soaking for me. She's always ready when I need her. Told you she's fucking perfect.

She's whimpering, making those sexy sounds, as I slide my finger against her wetness, making sure to press hard on her little nub. Her hips thrust back and forth, grinding against me, while we still kiss. It's not long until she's quivering under me and climaxes all over my fingers. Sexy as fuck.

I'm too impatient to take her to bed and fuck her. I need to have her right now. Sliding my zip down, I take out my rock hard cock, ripping away her lace. I pick her up, leaning her back against the bricks, thrusting inside her. She gasps and I stay still, feeling her warmth surrounding me. Sex has never felt like this before, even with Beth.

Gathering myself, so I don't blow my load too quickly, I begin to thrust inside her. Eve moans and whimpers as I pound into her. I've never wanted a girl to call me by my name during sex. When I asked her to last night, I was shocked by my own words. I love hearing her whimpering Angel as I bring her closer and closer to the edge, but it's my real name I want to hear on those soft plump lips of hers.

"Told you, Princess, to say my name when I'm inside you."

Her eyes widen a little, but she does as I say. "Gabe. Fuck me Gabe."

Yeah, that's more like it.

"Come for me baby. Give it to me."

"Oh my God, Gabe!" She falls apart, I follow right after.

***

After dressing Eve we head on back into the clubhouse. A party has started. I see Teresa and Prez heading our way and my arm goes around Eve.

Teresa grins at me. "Relax Angel. We're cool now."

I look down to Eve and she smiles. "I forgot to tell you."

Yeah, well that wasn't exactly our main focus ten minutes ago. Prez looks at my arm around Eve's waist, nodding a silent question to me. I answer with him with a nod of my own and he smiles. Fucker has probably being talking to Dragon.

We spend the rest of the night sitting around a table in the bar with Prez and Teresa. Seeing Eve happy with her friend again is great. I catch sight of Ink and stand.

"Angel?" Eve asks as Prez stands too.

"Come on VP you need to sort this with your brother."

Eve looks confused, but Teresa leans in close and whispers something to her. Prez slaps me on the back and we walk over to Ink, who's standing with a few of the other guys.

"Come for another shot VP?" Ink asks as soon as I get close.

"Enough." Prez growls. Loud enough to get Ink's attention, low enough that Eve doesn't hear. "Now listen here. You two better sort this shit right now. Ink, Angel's had Eve with him in his bed more than one night. He didn't have to claim her for you to know to back off. Angel, you should've let Ink know sooner if it wasn't clear. You both fucked up. We okay?"

Ink glares at me. "She know you claimed her?"

I nod. "She accepted."

I watch his face fall a little. Shit he really does like her.

"Treat her good Angel." He leans in, I return his hug and we slap each other on the back.

"With my life brother."

He nods and walks off.

When Eve looks like she's had enough to drink I take her back to my room. I should probably move back here now, I want to spend every night inside her.

***

Eve

Tonight's been pretty weird. I can't believe I agreed to Angel claiming me like that, but the truth is I love the caveman in him.

When Teresa told me that Angel had to go and make Ink understand I'm taken now, I felt a little bad for Ink.

I'm a little tipsy as Angel leads me back to my room. I start to become aroused anticipating what's going to happen, when we step inside.

Angel closes the door, locking it behind us before quickly grabbing me by the waist.

"You're mine now princess. Let me show you how I treat what's mine."

Chapter Eighteen

Eve

When I wake up I'm so sore, it feels heavenly. Last night was truly amazing, no it was marvelous! I let out a deep, satisfied sigh.

I can't think of a word to describe how great it was. You'll just have to take my word for it.

When we got back to the room last night, Angel showed me how he treated what was his. I was so wet and ready for him. He cherished me with dirty words, making me crumble as he gave me three orgasms. Yes he made me climax three fucking times! Last night was a little different too, maybe it was because we finally admitted we wanted each other. I had no doubt in my mind that I craved Angel, but when he told me about the meaning of claiming I was a goner. I know I'm walking a dangerous line here, but I can't stop myself taking that next step forward. I haven't said anything about what happens when I go back home, neither has he, it's going to happen eventually though. I don't know how I feel about that.

I feel his hard steel length pressing into my arse and giggle. Angel's large tattooed arms wrap around me and I feel a warmth settle over me. "Morning Princess."

He places a gentle kiss on my shoulder and I smile. "Morning Angel."

He grumbles something, then suddenly rolls me over on my back. Angel is on top of me, he's secured both of my hands in his above my head. "I told you to call me Gabe."

His eyes are deadly serious. I'm a little confused. "I thought that was just when we're having sex."

He shakes his head. "No baby. When we're alone, me and you. Whether we're just sitting together or I'm thrusting deep inside you, call me Gabe. I'm Gabe to you, no one else."

This is something serious, I'm left a little speechless. "Okay." I whisper.

He quirks one eyebrow at me and I smile. "Okay Gabe."

He grunts his approval. "That's more like it, Princess."

He kisses me like his life depends on it. I return it with just as much fervor. Angel's kisses are amazing, I could kiss him all day. Sadly he's got other plans, he leaves my mouth and I let out a small whine.

He chuckles. "Don't worry baby, I'm gonna make you feel real good."

I squirm at his words. I love how he talks to me. His kisses continue down my neck, giving me goose bumps. I'm sure all the hairs on my body are standing to attention. Angel trails his kisses down; when he gets to my breasts, he cruelly goes around the swell, never touching my nipples. I moan in frustration as his kisses move lower, below my belly button. My breathing hitches when he gets to my mound. I am soaking wet right now.

Angel stretches my legs open wider, diving in. I moan loudly as he devours me. When I said he's a good kisser, I didn't just mean on the mouth. Angel has a fucking talented mouth, right now though, I need more. I need him to be rough and take what he wants. Grabbing fistfuls of his hair I thrust my pussy into his face. "Fuck me Gabe."

I need more. I need him to fuck me now. "Gabe please."

He chuckles, kissing his way back up my body, when he reaches my mouth I can taste myself. It's enough to make me squirm under him. I feel his smooth tip at my entrance and I start to grind against it, trying to get some friction. Angel shows a little mercy, rubbing himself against my wetness. It feels great, but what I need is for him to put that cock in me.

I groan with frustration, but just as I do he eases himself into me. Angel is well hung, not only thick but long too, a delicious combination. He enters me, easing in gently so as not to hurt me. I'm still getting used to his size, douche-bag wasn't the biggest, and he definitely wasn't as thick as Angel.

Angel pushes further in, watching me. His eyes and his cock both drive me insane. My eyes roll back as he continues to enter me. Holy fuck! "Look at us Princess."

My eyes turn to him, confused as to what he means. He looks down to where we're joined, lifting my head I see Angel thrusting back and forth, his cock sinking into me and pulling back out, coated in my juices. Such an erotic image. Angel enters me a little faster now, a little deeper. My head falls back as I scream out. "Oh Gabe! Yes!"

I continue to pant, screaming his name as he fucks me harder. Grabbing my legs he throws them over his shoulder, sinking even deeper into me. I grip his wide shoulders for support as I start to fall into my orgasm. "Oh God, I'm gonna come Gabe!"

"Come with me baby. Now." He growls, releasing deep inside me. I feel myself shatter, tightening around him, milking him of everything he has to give me.

***

Gabe

Leaving Eve in bed this morning wasn't easy. I could have happily stayed there all day with her. Spending all day inside of her sounds like a fucking great day, but I'm heading to church for our final meeting. I'm sure Teresa will keep her busy with fucking wedding plans anyway.

The mood in the room is somber when I walk in. I feel their eyes on me as I enter. Our plan is risky, but we don't have any other choice, short of committing murder. We might sail close to the wind on occasion when it comes to keeping family safe. We've done a lot of shit, but we'd never strayed that far off the rails. Even for him. Besides, although I'd promised my mother I wouldn't hurt him, I never promised that someone else wouldn't. We've already made contact with guys who've been sent down because of him, and they can't wait to get their hands on him.

I greet the guys, taking my seat at the large table just as Prez walks into the room. He brings the meeting to order, looking to Disney for the first update.

The plan is fairly simple. Create a diversion at the Carnal compound gates. Hopefully that will cause enough of a distraction for Disney to sneak in and plant the drugs on Satan's bike. There's enough there to have him arrested for dealing. If the drugs on his bike aren't enough, we're also planting more at his house. Once we give our police contact the heads up, they'll head in and carry out their raids, putting Satan behind bars where he belongs.

Despite its simplicity, the plan has its risks. Carnal are always heavily armed, we'll need enough of a distraction at the front gates to make sure they're all out there, away from their bikes. Dragon and I will be responsible for that, under the guise of negotiating for Eve's safety. There's nothing I can think of that will get Satan to call off his dogs. If there was I would already have tried it. He's arrogant and cocky enough to want to put on a show for his club's benefit. I'm just hoping none of us get shot in the process. Or worse.

We've called in favors we didn't want to, to get this amount of drugs. They're being kept in a safe location away from the clubhouse for now. We'll have to be careful getting them over to Carnal or it'll be our guys who end up in jail instead. That would be all we fucking need right now.

We spend most of the day fine tuning the plan, ensuring every member knows where he needs to be and when. We work out the signal that'll let us know Disney's safely back out of the compound, then we decide where we'll all meet up again afterwards.

Everything's in place, but I can't shake the feeling we've missed something. The last thing we need is for it all to blow up in our faces. We've exhausted all other options though. Eve needs this from us, and every day we delay is another day our old ladies and families are at risk, thanks to Satan's threats.

Prez brings the meeting to a close, reminding everyone that tomorrow's his wedding day, and tonight we get drunk. We're not having a traditional bucks party out of respect for Elvis, but there's plenty of booze behind the bar and we plan to make a pretty big dent in it.

Dragon draws me aside before we leave the room. "You sure you're okay with this plan Angel? Seems to me that most of the risk is on you?"

I know he's worried for me, he's been more like a brother to me than my bastard twin ever was. I give him my confident shit eating grin, but I can tell he's not fooled. He puts on a brave face and we both pretend everything's okay, before heading to the bar to celebrate Prez's last night of freedom.

Chapter Nineteen

Eve

I wake up the next morning aching between my legs, a reminder of Angel's loving last night. When he said he wanted to be inside me every day he wasn't joking. Sex with him is so good, I can't get enough of it.

I turn to look at his sleeping form, relishing every inch of chiseled abs, firm legs and strong arms. Tracing the tattoos on his chest, I'm careful not to wake him. As much as I'd love another hot session with him, Teresa's got plans for me all day.

Reluctantly I draw back the sheets and head for the bathroom to shower.

When I emerge from the misty bathroom feeling refreshed, Angel's sitting up grinning at me. I walk over to my phone and call my daughter. It's late afternoon back home so she's a little tired, I keep the call short so she can go have her nap. When I hang up I'm a little teary. I miss her so fucking much it hurts.

Angel stands behind me, completely naked and pulls the towel off me. Wrapping his arms around me, kissing the back of my neck. "Come on, I'll make you feel better, Princess."

Although I'm probably going to get shit from Teresa for being late, I can't deny Angel.

***

The wedding was originally going to be a big affair, but out of respect we've toned down the plans and simplified it. Elvis wouldn't have wanted Teresa to call it off, but I think he'd approve of the changes we've made. The fairy tale styled dress has been returned, in its place is a simple white, floor length sheath dress that looks stunning on Teresa. She has the perfect figure for it. The back is almost non-existent and shows off her ink. In place of a princess tiara she has a diadem of fresh flowers in her hair. She looks beautiful.

My dress is a baby blue chiffon with fine straps and a sweetheart neckline. I've never seen my boobs look this good. I can't wait for Angel to see them. The hemline hovers just above my knees, long enough to be demure, yet short enough to give Angel a hard on when he sees my legs in these four inch strappy sandals.

Teresa looks at me, her head to one side. "You're thinking about sex again, you whore." she laughs.

I blush, she's right of course. I can't help it. Sex with Angel seems to have preoccupied my thoughts a lot these past few days. I don't think anyone would blame me really, if they knew how talented he is.

Teresa's holding a worn velvet jewel box in her hands, worrying at it. "What's that?" I question.

She opens the box slowly, revealing a gold locket in the shape of a heart, carefully passing it over to me. "It's my something old." She looks sad as she says this. "It belonged to my mum, dad gave it to her on their wedding day."

Damn, she looks like she's about to cry. I swallow the lump in my throat. "Don't you bloody cry." I admonish. "I've done your make up once, I'm not doing it again."

I'm not sure just how waterproof this mascara is. She smiles and I take the locket, moving over to Teresa, who lifts her long hair out of the way for me to fasten it around her neck. It's perfect. She places her hand over it and smiles. I know she's thinking about Elvis and her mum.

We run through the checklist. Something old - the locket... something new - the dress... something borrowed - a delicate lace handkerchief from Diane... something blue - a lace garter... and a sixpence in her shoe. I'd brought the sixpence over from England with me, I'd found it in a gorgeous little gift shop one afternoon.

Teresa stands, and the full effect of the dress is stunning. I think I prefer this simpler design, it's certainly a lot more flattering on her slender frame than her original choice. It looks so out of place in this room, with its masculine furniture and decor. We should have been getting ready at her house, but Prez made this one demand for today, claiming he couldn't keep us safe there.

The service will still go ahead at the Church, but the reception has been moved to the Clubhouse rather than the fancy hotel that was booked. In some ways I think this revised wedding is a better fit for Prez and Teresa, it feels more suited to their biker lifestyle than the princess style wedding she'd originally planned.

***

There's a horrible sense of déjà vu as we pull up outside the church, although this time I'm sharing the car with Teresa, Sue and Diane. Sue reaches for Teresa's hand and she holds mine as we make our way over to

Elvis's grave. Teresa wanted to talk to her dad on the day of her wedding. I love her even more for it. After Teresa had finally stopped blaming me for the death of her father, Sue and I had a talk too. She couldn't stop apologizing for what she'd said to me, when I came by to see her after the funeral. Thankfully everything's on track with us all now. Once Teresa has said her heart felt words, she turns to face us, her eyes red rimmed with unshed tears. Sue gives her a gentle hug. "Your dad would be so proud of you today girl. You look so beautiful."

Luckily Diane breaks the sad mood. "Come on sweetie, sooner we get you married, the sooner you can have hot monkey sex with your husband."

I can't believe she just said that, trust Diane to equate the day with sex, but it worked. The mood has lifted and we're all wearing huge grins. I wait in the vestibule with Teresa, while Diane and Sue go ahead and take their seats. We've agreed that I'll start walking down the aisle ahead of her, and she'll follow behind on her own. It wouldn't have felt right asking anyone else to give her away.

I hear the opening bars of the song she's chosen to walk down the aisle to, my eyes start misting up. I start to make my way down the aisle to *The Wonder of You* by Elvis. Teresa chose it because it's a beautiful love song, it makes her feel like Elvis is here with her, still taking part. I feel like he's watching as well as I begin to walk to the lyrics of the song. At the front of the church, on the left of the aisle, there's the photo of Elvis laughing. Armageddon is one of mine and Teresa's favourite movies. The wedding scene at the end, where the photos are at the front of the church in place of the loved ones who'd not come home really touched us. It just seemed right somehow to do the same. I smile at his picture.

Prez looks nervous, shuffling on his feet. I can see the exact moment he spots Teresa; his whole face lighting up with love, he suddenly stands tall and stops fidgeting. To his right stands Angel, and I'm not ashamed to say my face heats up with lust. I'm pretty sure I see it reciprocated on his face. They're not wearing traditional suits, would you have really expected them to? They're all dressed pretty much the same, black trousers, black buttoned shirts, and their cuts. Angel looking slightly smarter than usual has my tongue salivating. I give myself a mental shake, this is not the time for getting horny, it's my best friend's wedding, for fuck's sake. Pulling myself together I make it to the end of the aisle, taking my place on the left, radiating happiness as I see Angel give me a wink.

***

The service was emotional and beautiful. They'd written their own vows. I noticed Teresa didn't include obey in hers, that would have been an impossible task, although she did include worshiping his body on a daily basis, that had us all laughing. That's my girl.

We're back at the clubhouse, the food eaten, the cake cut, and they've just had their first dance. It's been a long day, but when Angel pulls me to my feet to dance to *I Don't Want To Miss A Thing* by Aerosmith, I can't wait to be in his arms. The song is perfect for how I'm feeling right now, I don't want to close my eyes and miss a moment of this short time I have left with Angel. He draws me closer as we move around the dance floor.

After that dance with Angel the music changed to something more upbeat, and we started dirty dancing. Between the drinks I've consumed and spending the whole night practically dry humping each other, we're both worked up and horny as fuck.

We say our goodbyes to Teresa and Prez, before Angel pulls me in the direction of our room.

As soon as we step inside Angel is all over me. "Fuck! You look hot as fuck in this dress."

I whimper as he takes control. Angel likes to be in charge and I love letting him have that control. It turns me on to be dominated by him.

He pulls back from our kiss and literally rips the beautiful dress from me. It lands with a swoosh on the floor, I definitely heard it tear. Angel shrugs arrogantly. "I'll fix that later."

He moves us to stand in front of the floor length mirror in the corner of the room. He stands behind me fully dressed while I'm in just my underwear. He places his hands on my shoulders as we look at each other through our reflection. "You need to know how sexy you are."

I blush as he kisses the crook of my neck. "Look at yourself, Eve."

I do as he says, but I don't see what he sees. I see a normal, average looking girl looking back at me.

Angel eases away my bra and thong. I squirm at the sight of my reflection. I've always been naturally slim, with a bigger bottom, my breasts drooping a little from breast feeding, my belly showing stretch marks; they're there because of my baby and I'm proud of them.

Angel rains kisses down my spine and growls. "Fucking beautiful."

He walks away, leaving me standing alone, watching him as he strolls over to a table in the other corner. He picks it up and places it in front of me. "Bend over."

I do as he says, feeling his hand on my back, guiding me slowly down. When my breasts are touching the hard table Angel rubs his hands over my arse cheeks and I shiver. "I want you to look at yourself Eve."

I raise my head to look at him behind me. He shakes his head, pointing to the mirror. "Watch yourself in the mirror. I want you to see how fucking sexy you are."

He slowly undresses, never taking his eyes from mine. When he's standing behind me naked and glorious he nudges my legs further apart, sliding his finger through my pussy from behind. I moan quietly at the sensation. When I see Angel bring his finger to his mouth and lick my juices my eyes widen. Why is he teasing me like this?

He flashes me his cocky grin, gripping onto my waist. "Don't take your eyes off the mirror." he warns before he enters me. This feels divine. He takes it slow for a couple of thrusts to allow me to adjust to his size, then continues to push deeper. I watch my face in the mirror as I take what he has to give me. My eyes are shining, my cheeks flushed. When I think Angel is all the way in he surprises me by thrusting deeper. He hits places that trigger a passion frenzy inside of me. My face completely changes as Angel pushes all the way in, fucking me into oblivion. I hardly recognize the girl in front of me.

My gaze stays on the mirror as Angel fucks me from behind. My face is lit up with pleasure. I reach back with my hand, flicking my clit, gasping on the edge. This is the best, *pant*, sex, *moan*, ever, *scream*!

After we have both satisfied our hunger for each other, Angel picks me up and carries me to the bed. My legs feel too much like jelly to walk anyway. He gets in beside me, pulling me to him so I fit perfectly against him and I fall asleep.

Chapter Twenty

Gabe

Leaving Eve this morning was hard. I know she'll give me shit for not waking her and saying goodbye, but I want to remember that peaceful look she has on her face whilst she's sleeping. She doesn't know what's happening today, none of the old ladies do. If she'd seen my face she would have known something serious was going down today. We've all tried to keep a lid on it around our families because this plan can fuck up in our faces fast. If Eve sensed what I was about to do, I think she'd try to stop me and that's never going to happen. Once it's voted on its set, I don't want an argument before I set off, and I save us from it by leaving quietly.

We head out of the compound on our bikes. There are two groups, the guys coming with me to the compound, the others going with Cowboy to plant the rest of the drugs at Satan's house. With a nod of the head we separate. Normally I'd be enjoying the ride, but there's just too much at stake today. I feel like I'm going through the motions. Because of all this shit I haven't had chance to take Eve out on the back of my bike again.

Disney and his guys pull off down a side road; we stop to wait for the signal that tells us they're in place. The text comes through less than five minutes later. It's show time. We cruise to the front of the Carnal compound; we agreed there should only be four of us, me, Dragon and a couple of prospects. We don't want to have a show of force, as far as these guys are concerned I'm here to barter for Eve's life not start a war.

The guard on the gate draws in a breath as he recognizes me and Dragon. It's not exactly hard, I look exactly like his VP. "Never thought I'd see the day you stupid fuckers showed up here." He sneers, he's armed and makes a show of cocking his gun in my direction. Yeah, we all have guns here dipshit.

"Shut the fuck up and get my brother out here." I command, bored of his shit already. My voice sounds a heck of a lot stronger than I'm feeling. "We need to talk business."

I look the guard up and down, showing my contempt. He picks up his phone and speaks into it; from where we are outside the gates, I can't hear what's being said. He receives an answer that surprises him from the look on his face. "He'll be out in a minute, says for you to stay that side of the gates with your guns where we can see them."

It's only moments before he's joined by armed back up. I see my brother strutting towards me, arrogance oozing from him. Apart from getting a little glimpse of him that day at Frank's store, I haven't seen him in years. I know it sounds fucking stupid but fuck me we're identical. Apart from the cut he's wearing, his tattoos and the frown that is. I hold in my smile because true to plan, he walks out with what looks like the rest of his club following him.

Shit's begun.

"What the fuck do you want?" Satan struts up to the gate, his leather cut swinging open revealing the ink all over his chest. His gun hangs loosely at the end of his arm, obviously not considering me a threat worth worrying about. Perfect.

"I've come to make a deal." My voice is calm, free of emotion. He'll hate that. He's never been happy unless I was hurting.

His frown deepens. "Unless you've come to hand the girl over, we've got nothing to talk about." He looks behind me, checking whether we brought Eve with us or not.

His eyes go hard when he realizes she's not here. I notice the grip on his guns tightens. "I made it very clear I want that girl, or I'm going to fuck with every one of your old ladies and whores. I know some of your guys have kids too." He ends with a grin. I would like nothing better than to put a bullet through his fucking head right now, but that's not the plan. That would start a war and, with only four of us here, it would be a war we would lose.

"You know I can't hand her over to you, brother. That's a death sentence for her. There's got to be something we can offer to avoid that happening." I stare him down and wait. There's no way this fucker will deal, he knows it and I know it. He shakes his head, quickly looking to his President then back at me. Scalp has been the President of Carnal for a long time now. As corrupted as his club is I was still a little surprised when he patched in my brother. If I know Satan, then I've a feeling he has something over him, allowing Satan to make all the decisions. Maybe we should have approached Scalp first.

"There's nothing you can offer me." He sneers. "I want the girl, and I want her today or I carry out my promise. The club whores around here are getting boring, same old pussy, I need something new."

There's no emotion in his eyes at all, just cold steel reflected back at me. "Severed pussy will do just as well as the whores around here." He adds.

I see Dragon give me the nod. Disney's safely out and back at the meeting point. Careful not to show the relief in my eyes I turn back to Satan. Saying the first thing that comes to my mind. "What happened to you? You broke our mothers heart you know that?"

Shit. As soon as the words come out of my mouth, I knew I shouldn't have mentioned her. His face changes in an instant. "Don't you fucking talk to me about our mother!" He yells, taking a step forward. "She never fucking loved me! It was always about you. Gabe this, Gabe that, why the fuck couldn't I be more like Gabe?" He's so angry he's spitting the words in my direction. The words he's shouting are childish, but that's where his hate stems from. He's always hated whatever I had.

He looks at me with so much hatred in his eyes, I already know what's coming next, the gun in his hand is rising to point directly at me. It happens so quickly I don't have time to react. A burning pain hits me right in the chest and I go down. I surrender to the blackness, the sounds of gun fire and the memory of Eve's face as she slept this morning my last conscious thoughts.

***

Dragon

What the fuck just happened?

All hell let loose around here. Shots are being fired left right and fucking centre. Angel's on the ground, blood everywhere. Fuck! The only satisfaction I have is that I managed to hit his fucker of a brother, Satan. I hope I fucking killed him, evil prick.

While our prospects lay down covering fire I drag Angel over to my bike. Between us we haul him over the tank and I get the fuck out of there. As I pull away the two prospects join me, one riding Angel's bike. Doesn't matter if we're being shot at, Angel will fucking kill me if I leave his bike. With both prospects by my side we race away. We don't get far when I notice one of them freeze and fall from his bike. Those bastards fucking shot him in the back! We don't have time to stop for him, we have to get Angel out of here. I need to get him back to Doc as soon as fucking possible. I can't tell if he's breathing or not, so I speed up and head back to the meeting point as fast as I can, knowing Doc will be there. He'd agreed to come along just in case it all went tits up, and it has.

The meeting point is far enough to be safe, but close enough that they've heard the gun fire. The guys are milling around nervously as I pull up. Doc rushes over as soon as he sees Angel laid over my bike. Fuck, I hope I'm in time.

**

After Doc quickly looks Angel over he looks up at me, shaking his head and I stop breathing. "It's bad." He mutters. Cowboy's group was successful and has joined us. We're all quiet, waiting to hear Angel's fate. "I can't fix this here, we need to get him to the hospital now."

I look at him, not daring to voice the question but he answers anyway. "I don't know Dragon, right now it could go either way. He's lost a fuck load of blood. I've stopped it for now, but I don't know what damage the bullet's done. It's still in there and it's close to his heart."

"Fuck, get that truck over here now!" Disney's the first to respond, driving the truck over to where Angel lays bleeding on the ground. We place him in the back of the truck as carefully as we can, Doc stays with him, keeping pressure on the wound. I jump into the front seat, pulling my phone from my pocket as we race to the hospital. I turn back to look at Angel, he's deathly white, I can't see him breathing but Doc just nods. Letting me know he's still with us. Sighing deeply I open the phone, bringing up Prez's number. Time to report in to the boss.

Chapter Twenty One

Eve

I was pissed this morning. I woke up to find Angel had left without a word. He'd muttered something about club business last night, before I fell asleep, but I hadn't paid attention. I don't know how long he's been gone, if he's going to be gone all day or walk back in at any minute. I try reminding myself this is just sex, there's no relationship here, but it's fucking hard. The way he looks at me like I'm the centre of his world, has me melting. Nobody's ever looked at me like that, and the way he talks to me. Not just caveman biker, he talks to me like I'm a real woman. I think I've fallen big time for this bad ass biker. Shit that wasn't supposed to happen.

It's already late morning by the time I've showered and dressed and spent five minutes talking to my baby girl. I head out to see if there's any food on the go. I need to start watching what I'm eating around here, the women dish up huge meals for the members and do the same for everyone else. I don't want to be going home carrying extra weight.

I'm surprised to see Teresa eating breakfast at the kitchen counter. I'd not expected her to emerge from her hot wedding night sexcapade until much later. She nods her head in greeting, her mouth too full of frosted flakes to allow her to talk. She looks tired so I guess she was kept up all night, as she should.

"Morning." I greet her, she gives me a mumble in response. "I didn't expect you to be out of bed yet, that hot husband of yours should have you under him having some hot morning sex." I laugh.

Teresa gives me a disgusted look. "Fucking club business." She mutters. "He's been on edge all fucking morning, won't tell me what's going on." She takes a deep breath, "He did keep me up all night though," she adds with a devilish grin.

Whatever's happening must be important as there's hardly any of the guys around. It's not usually busy this time in the morning, but there's normally a few guys lounging around or digging into whatever's being served. From what I can see there's only a few prospects and Prez who's in his office.

Diane walks in, looking tired and greets us both. "Hey sweeties. Why aren't you two still in bed having hot sex with your men?" she laughs, bumping her hip into me.

"Same goes to you." I laugh.

"Dragon was off at the bloody crack of dawn." she sulks. "He kept me up all night then the fucker woke me at stupid o'clock to say goodbye." She looks less than impressed.

I pass her the coffee I've just made and busy myself making a fresh cup for me. It seems to perk her up and she turns to Teresa. "So tell me about all the hot sex last night!"

Teresa almost chokes on her cereal, blushing. I've never seen Teresa blush before, especially not over sex. That must have been some night.

Just as she's about to spill the beans, there's an almighty roar from the office followed by the sound of smashing. We all rush out to see what's happening. When we reach the office we see the door practically hanging from its hinges, the chairs overturned. Prez is standing in the middle of the room holding the phone in his hand. His face goes white as he sees us.

"What the fuck is going on?" Teresa asks him.

"The plan went to shit." He slumps to the sofa, pulling Teresa onto his lap. "They shot him, baby." He whispers but we all hear it. "The fuckers shot him."

There's silence in the room, we're all wondering who he's talking about, and what the fuck is going on.

"Who got shot?" Diane asks, her lips drawn tightly into a grimace. Prez doesn't answer her, he doesn't answer any of us. "Who the fuck got shot, Prez?" she screams at him.

Prez looks up, seeking out my face, and in that moment I know. "It's Angel."

My legs shake and my head spins before my world goes black.

Chapter Twenty Two

Dragon

Disney's pacing up and down the waiting room. I'm surprised he hasn't worn a path between the coffee machine and the nurses' station. It's fucking grating on my nerves, I don't ask him to stop though, as I know he's feeling this as much as I am. All of the brothers are feeling it. The nurse at the desk looks uncomfortable, as she would with a waiting room of scary looking bikers, I suppose. Doc is talking to her, trying to find out what's happening with Angel, from the look of frustration on his face she's not telling him much.

The door to the ER opens and a doctor walks out. His scrubs are covered in blood, Angel's blood. He spots Doc, they obviously know each other. We all stand as he moves towards us. "How is he?" Doc questions.

The doctor spouts some medical bullshit we don't understand, so we all look at Doc and wait for him to explain. "They're taking him into surgery" he tells us. "They've managed to stabilize the bleeding, but they need to get the bullet out and repair some of the damage." He breathes in slowly. "He's not out of the woods yet. If he makes it through the surgery there's a good chance he'll make a full recovery, but right now he's lost a shit load of blood and he's in bad shape."

"He's a fighter Doc, of course he'll pull through." I reassure the guys. I hope to fuck I'm right, I can't lose Angel. He's like my brother.

***

Eve

I feel something cold on my forehead and I struggle to open my eyes. I see Diane holding a wet cloth against me. What the fuck? Then the memory comes rushing back and I gasp. Angel's been shot!

"Take it easy." Diane cautions."You dropped like a stone sweetie." She pats my arm and I swat her away.

"Where is he Prez?" I plead. "I need to see him, please." My voice is breaking. Fuck, so is my heart.

Prez gathers us together, promising to take us to the hospital. There's been no further news whilst I've been unconscious. No news is good news right?

***

The waiting room is full of club members when we get there. Diane rushes over to Dragon, gasping when she sees how much blood he's covered in. "It's okay baby," he reassures her "it's not my blood, I'm okay". Diane falls onto him, sobbing, pulling him tightly to her. I don't think she wants to let him out of her sight.

I stare at what must be Angel's blood covering him, watching Dragon pull Prez into a corner, presumably to fill him in. Shit, the look on Prez's face isn't good. What the fuck's been happening today? There's a heated conversation between them, before Prez heads back over to Teresa and me to fill us in. He draws me over to the seating area, pushing me down onto the cold plastic seat. I tense as I wait for him to give me the news I've been dreading all the way here.

"He's in surgery Eve, they've still got to get the bullet out. We've just got to wait and see what the surgeon says." He looks broken.

Teresa sits down next to me, drawing me close. It's a waiting game.

***

We sit in the hospital for hours. Nobody wants to leave, especially me. The guys head outside for a smoke once in a while, but come back in to resume their silent pacing. I stay put, too afraid to move. Some of the men have tried to talk to me, but I'm not exactly in a talkative mood right now. Even Ink tried. I haven't really had the chance to speak to him since that night. I should have really, I feel bad that I didn't spot the signs earlier, but at the moment I'm not in a place to want to sit and chat. All I can manage to give him is a weak smile right now.

Teresa stays by my side the whole time and I'm thankful. I'm clutching a cold coffee in a death grip. It's an insult to call it a coffee. It tastes more like stale cigarette ash in hot water, still it's a distraction for my hands. Diane is curled up in Dragon's lap. She's still not letting him go, I don't blame her.

Disney keeps looking at his phone, like it's going to give him the answers that we're all seeking. I wish.

Suddenly his phone sounds an alert and he signals for Prez and Dragon. I watch as they follow each other outside. I catch Teresa looking at me and she shrugs her shoulders. It figures they would go and talk away from the ears of the women.

When they return Disney has a huge grin on his face. What the fuck?

Prez pulls the guys into a corner and fills them in, they're too far away for us to hear. Whatever he says has them all smiling just like Dragon. A couple of them slap each other on the back. I'm more confused than ever. How can you look that happy at a time like this?

***

Finally a doctor comes through the doors and heads straight towards us, his face grim. He walks over to Prez and I slowly stand, steeling myself for the bad news I'm expecting.

"He's going to be okay." The doctor wastes no time in telling us. I sag with relief and Disney reaches for me to hold me up. Prez does the same to Teresa and Dragon's holding Diane close to him. "He's going to be in a lot of pain so we're keeping him sedated for now, but we've repaired the damage and taken out the bullet fragments."

The Doctor keeps talking but I don't hear him, his words have blurred together. All I can hear are the words, "He's going to be okay." Repeating in my head, the relief is indescribable. I really thought I'd lost him.

Prez motions to me to come closer."Doc here says you can go sit with him if you want."

Oh yes, I do want. Prez tells me he's only allowed two visitors, so it's just me and him following the doctor down the hallway. Once Prez has seen that Angel is fine, Dragon wants to come and check up on him. The doctor leads us down a maze of corridors before stopping outside a door, motioning us in. I slowly walk into the sterile white room, stopping in my tracks. I hardly recognize the man lying in the bed. He's so pale, not his usual tan. There are wires and tubes everywhere. I draw in a gasp at the sight of him.

The doctor touches my arm gently. "It looks worse than it is now. The tubes should be gone by the morning as we wean him off the sedation." He motions to a chair at the side of the bed. "Go sit with him, hold his hand and talk to him. It helps."

I don't move straight away so Prez places a hand on my shoulder, guiding me over to the chair. I pick up Angel's hand in mine, holding back a sob; now isn't the time for this. My man needs me to be strong for him. I realize what I just referred to him as. My man. It feels good. I do what the doctor said. I sit in the chair, holding his hand and talk nonsense for the rest of the night.

Chapter Twenty Three

Gabe

What the fuck is that beeping noise?

It's starting to piss me off. I can feel something warm in my hand and my throat fucking kills. I try and open my eyes, but it's a fight. I'm not a quitter so I finally manage to get them open. After my eyes have adjusted and I'm no longer squinting, I get my first look around.

Everything is white. Where the fuck am I?

I'm laid in a bed and my shoulder hurts like fuck. I struggle to find a memory to tell me how I got here. I start to remember, seeing the look on Satan's face as he lifted his gun, aiming it right at me. The fucker.

I hear a sigh next to me and it reminds me of the warm feeling in my hand. My body's a little sore and weak, so I struggle to move my head. Shit that hurt, every movement sends a shock to my shoulder. When I see Eve in the chair that's pulled up close to the side of the bed, I relax. Her head is laid on the covers, her hand grasping mine and she's fast asleep.

I wiggle my fingers in her hand and feel her body tense. Her eyes shoot open, her gaze fixing straight on me. Fuck, she's the most beautiful sight in the world. It takes her a couple of seconds to react, when she does she immediately sits upright. "Gabe?" She's looking at me in awe. "Oh my God, Gabe, I thought I'd lost you!"

Shit, now she's crying and I can't move to comfort her. I grasp her hand tightly, trying to talk but I can't, there's something in my throat. What the fuck is that?

"Wait, don't try and talk yet. I'll get a nurse."

Nurse? Eve quickly runs to the door, shouting for a nurse. A matronly looking figure walks in and approaches the bed at a measured pace. Eve doesn't seem to appreciate her slow gait and shouts at her again, rushing her along. If I could I would laugh. Fucking cute. The nurse talks calmly to me. I find out that I've been here for nearly twenty-four hours between my surgery and sleeping. I'm fucking shocked! Apparently I've got a tube shoved down my throat, she explains everything as she removes it.

After it's removed I glare at her. Sharp fucking scratch? Bitch, that fucking hurt.

My throat feels raw. The nurse places an ice chip on my tongue and I gratefully suck on it, cooling the burning sensation. She reminds me not to talk too much for the rest of the day and most of tomorrow; apparently it can damage my voice box. I see Eve pacing up and down the small room, fussing with her hands whilst the nurse carries out the rest of her checks, telling me the doctor will be in soon. As soon as she leaves, Eve's back at my side. She takes hold of my hand, turning it in her own. There are tears rolling down her face. Before we can talk we're interrupted by the door opening, it's Prez. His face lights up when he sees I'm awake.

"You scared the fucking shit out of us, you fucker!" Relief washes across his face, "I'm so glad you're okay mate!"

I try and talk but nothing comes out. Eve places another ice cube in my mouth, telling me off for trying to talk. When it's cooled my throat I manage to rasp "What the fuck happened?" looking to Prez for answers.

He looks a little shocked at the sound of my voice. "You got yourself shot you stupid shit." he laughs. He knows I was asking for more of an answer than that, so he continues. "It's all good, Disney got word the raid went ahead and they've got Satan in custody. Cops found everything and managed to find some other shit they wanted him for. Dragon managed to shoot the fucker. He's got a flesh wound but he'll survive. Fucking shame."

He sounds disappointed at that last bit of news. I manage to smile at him. "Casualties?"

"We lost one of the prospects. Carnal fuckers shot him in the back."

Eve gasps, she's sitting listening to Prez talk. Obviously this is all news to her. "Everyone else is fine.", Prez reassures me.

I grasp Eve's hand more tightly. "It's okay Princess." I falter on the last part, due to a combination of pain and emotion. As if sensing my pain Eve reaches over, placing another cube of ice onto my tongue. It worked. The plan worked. Eve should be safe now, and it feels like a huge weight has been lifted from me at the thought. Now all I have to figure out is how to persuade Eve to get her daughter out here and make them stay. Eve has to stay here, with me.

***

The doctor checks the dressing on my wound and seems happy enough. "Looking good. I'll have another look tomorrow and, if all goes well, you could be home in a couple of days."

He smiles at me before he goes, leaving me pissed. I don't know what he's so happy about. I want to get the fuck out of this place, but he's just told me I've got to stay here. That isn't good fucking news.

I'm propped up in the bed, trying to get comfortable on this hard as shit bed, when Eve walks back in. One of the nurses took pity on her, and showed her where she could grab a shower and freshen up. She looks a lot more comfortable now, even if she is wearing yesterday's clothes. I told her to go back to the clubhouse and get herself sorted, but she gave me a dirty look and told me no. I didn't mention it again.

"Hey Princess." I pat the bed beside me and she comes and sits down, leaning over and giving me a slow, sensual kiss. Shit, I'm hard for her already. It never takes long with Eve, if I'm honest; my dick's always semi hard when she's near me. Before I can do anything to take care of it the door opens, Dragon and Prez walking in. It's like Central fucking station in here this morning.

"Morning fucker." Dragon greets me. "You scared the shit out of me yesterday brother!"

I can imagine. I still see Elvis's face staring at me covered in blood when I close my eyes. I'd hate Dragon to have memories like that.

"What's the news?" I ask as Prez shuts the door before moving closer to the bed.

"They've denied him bail. Looks like the plan worked. They're moving him to the detention centre later today. Lot of fuckers in there can't wait to get their hands on him."

I should feel something shouldn't I? After all he's my blood, my twin, but instead I just feel relief that it's over. Eve's going to be safe now. I can claim her as my old lady. We can finally get out of the clubhouse, I can have her on the back of my bike. I look to Eve and see she's looking shocked and pale. I'm not sure how much of this the guys have explained to her.

"You're safe now Princess." I rub the back of her hand. "It's all going to be okay now baby."

***

Eve

I sit there, my head switching between Prez and Angel as they're talking. I'm struggling to take in what they're saying. I can hear Angel telling me it's over, but he's lying in a hospital bed because of me. He almost died because of me. I'm a fucking curse to the people around me. Ever since I got here I've brought nothing but trouble and grief to everyone.

It registers that somehow Satan has been arrested, yet I don't feel the relief that I should. Something just doesn't feel right about all of this. I look back to Angel and realize that somewhere along this mad journey I fell in love with him. When I thought I was going to lose him last night it almost destroyed me. I know that being with Angel will never be sweetness and roses. I'd almost convinced myself that I could settle for the hot and hard sex with him, but then I let my fucking emotions get in the way.

I start to panic, I need to get out of here. "I need to go find Teresa." I mumble, not sure if they've even stopped talking. I snatch my hand from Angel and ignore his questions as I hurry from the room.

I need my best friend right now. I need her to talk to me and make sense of all this mess in my head because I sure as fuck can't do it on my own. "I'll be back later, I'm glad you're going to be okay." I throw over my shoulder without looking back. I can't look back.

***

Gabe

What the fuck just happened?

Eve freaked out and shot out of here like a bat out of hell. I'll never understand women. I look to Prez and Dragon, they just shrug their shoulders, they've not got a fucking clue either.

"When are they letting you out of here?" Dragon's picked up my chart from the end of the bed and is squinting at it. As if he understands a word that's written on there. I barely understand half of what the doctors say to me, never mind the shit they've written down about me. Prez snatches it from him and shakes his head as he puts it back.

"Doctor said a couple of days." I grumble. Fuck that, I want to get out now. Dragon and Prez exchange an odd look. What's that about? "What's up guys?"

Dragon looks uncomfortable as he answers. "Eve's flying home tomorrow, remember? With Satan inside there's no reason for her not to go home. You told her how you feel about her yet?"

Dragon knows me too well. Of course he knows I haven't told her how I feel.

"Shit!" I curse. "Get me a fucking Doctor, I need to get out of this place now."

Dragon goes off to find one. I don't care if I have to crawl out of this place on my fucking hands and knees, I'm getting out of here. I need to go tell Eve that she's not going anywhere.

Chapter Twenty Four

Eve

I'm sitting in the bedroom back at the clubhouse, feeling guilty as hell. I can't believe I ran out of the hospital like that. Teresa looked surprised to see me when I walked through the clubhouse door. She'd expected me to stay at the hospital with Angel. It's where I should be, but I can't bring myself to do it. I gave her some feeble excuse about needing a quick nap, rushing off to hide in my room.

The closer it gets to my time to leave, the harder it's going to be to let him go. I have to let him go. My flight home is booked for tomorrow. Whilst Satan was a threat I'd understood I couldn't go home on my scheduled flight, but now he's been arrested there's no longer a reason to stay.

I can't afford to swap my ticket, and I'm missing Elizabeth too much. Hot sex with Angel just isn't a good enough reason to stay. Taking a chance on Angel, hoping that something might come of this relationship isn't a gamble I can take as a mother. Since he claimed me, we've hardly spoken about it, I don't know where I stand. It's understandable that he wanted to claim me for my stay here, I don't like to share either.

Angel's going to be in the hospital for a couple of more days, so I'll need to go back and say my goodbye to him this evening. I'll need some Dutch courage before I go so I leave the sanctuary of my room. I head straight for the bar, hoping a couple of shots will make this easier.

Most of the guys are in the bar, celebrating now that Angel has pulled through. It's not quite a full blown party, they're still in mourning over Elvis, but they need to kick back and celebrate yesterday's success.

I'm greeted warmly by everyone I pass. These guys really do make me feel like I'm part of this family, it's a great feeling. One I could get used to and I'm going to miss, but how will it feel when Angel grows tired of me?

The longer I stay here the more it will hurt. I can justify leaving as often as I want, but the thought of it still makes me feel like shit.

My place is back home in England with my daughter. Why the fuck did I have to fall in love with a man thousands of miles away and in a different fucking time zone? There's no way of making this work. I wish I'd just had longer to work out how I felt, to know that I'm making the right decision rather than gambling and possibly giving up my only chance at happiness. This situation is shit.

One of the prospects is behind the bar and I ask for a shot of vodka. The neat alcohol burns my throat as it makes it way down, but I welcome it. I turn and survey the room behind me as he pours a second shot. Diane and Dragon are cuddled up together in the far corner. I know yesterday she went through hell not knowing if it was her husband who'd been shot. It looks like she's keeping her man close. From the way her hands are all over his body I'm not sure if she's checking for injuries or just good old fashioned groping. Who am I kidding? She'll definitely be having a good grope, they enjoy their public displays. I can't help smiling at these two, it's obvious they love each other deeply, and they're good for each other. Their personalities fit and I envy them.

Growing up I never got to see relationships that worked. The only example I had was Elvis and Babs, but they weren't into PDA's.

Teresa is nestled on Prez's lap. She looks blissful. I'm so happy for my friend. Now all of this shit is over and I'm going home they'll be able to go on their delayed honeymoon. She'd refused to go and leave me here by myself. I feel good that I'm going home knowing she's happy and safe. Although she lost Elvis, she's got a man who loves her and a family who'll fight for her. I'm going to miss her so much again.

I see Cowboy dancing with one of the club whores. He winks at me when he sees me watching. The guys all look so much more relaxed after the stress of the last few weeks. I didn't realize at first that from the moment I came here things changed for the worse for them. Now the danger is over it's great to see them being themselves.

Doc is sitting with Sue at one of the tables and beckons me over. "How's Angel doing?"

I sit with them and relate as much as I can remember from the nurses' visits while I was at the hospital.

"He's still in a lot of pain." I laugh as I recall how much of a baby he can be over having an injection, yet how much of a grizzly he is when it comes to hiding the pain he's feeling. "They've told him if he behaves he could be home in a couple of days."

"That's great news." Doc says. "I really thought we were going to lose him yesterday you know." His face falls at the memory. I pat his hand reassuringly.

"You did a great job Doc, you kept him alive 'till you got to the hospital." Angel owes his life to this man. I'm not sure anyone's told Angel just how badly injured he was.

Sue looks over at me. "I thought you'd have been at the hospital with him?" She sounds surprised that I'm not.

"I was so drained I needed a nap. There was nowhere I could get comfortable at the hospital. Angel told me to get back here and rest. I'm going to head back shortly."

Did that sound believable? They seem to buy it. I wonder if Prez and Dragon said anything about my sudden departure.

"Are you still planning on flying home tomorrow?" she asks.

I nod and she looks disappointed. I can't seem to get any words out so mutter something about a drink and make a move, dashing back to the bar.

I'm downing my second shot of Vodka, resigning myself to heading back to the hospital to say my farewell when the front door opens. Angel walks in, causing me to start choking on my drink as it goes down the wrong way. He looks over to me, his warm smile swiftly changing to a look of concern as I choke. Before he can reach me, Cowboy's already there, patting me on my back.

"Take it easy babe." He laughs. "You Brits can't handle your drink."

Once he sees I'm okay he gives me a quick hug before heading back to his dance partner, laughing at me all the way. I see Angel try and make his way towards me but before he can he's quickly surrounded by his brothers. All happy to see him but concerned over his early release and his state of health. Doc guides him over to the table he's sharing with Sue, helping him to sit down. I see Angel is now deathly pale and in a lot of pain I'm guessing. Stubborn man won't say he's in pain though.

His eyes search me out, and I move towards him slowly. "What the fuck are you doing back here Angel?" Doc doesn't sound happy at all. "Not that I'm not pleased to see you, but shit, you're in no fit state to be released."

All eyes turn to Angel. "I couldn't stay in that place Doc." He whines. "They didn't have any decent whiskey." Typical Angel, everyone breaks out laughing at his reply. Doc still looks concerned though and Angel takes pity on him. "I signed myself out against medical advice. We both know I'll heal better here and it's not like I don't have my own Doc on call." He cheekily smirks.

He reaches for me. "Eve can take care of me." He pulls me closer. He can sense that I'm scared of hurting him so reassures me. "It's okay Princess, you won't hurt me. Seeing you makes me feel better."

Sue laughs. "You high VP?"

Doc turns to me. "You got a minute Eve?" Angel is reluctant to let me go, but I follow him anyway as Angel slowly releases me.

Doc and I move to a quieter corner of the room where we can talk without shouting. "He's too bloody stubborn for his own good." He mutters, not looking happy at all. I simply nod in agreement, I'm not sure what Doc needs me for. "Do you think you could persuade him to go back to his room and rest?" He asks.

"Of course I will, do you need me to stay with him?"

"I think that would help keep him calm." He looks over at Angel for a second before returning his gaze to mine. "I'm going to give him a sedative, I'll tell him it's just a strong painkiller, but he needs knocking out if he's going to get any sleep tonight. He'd refuse point blank if he knew what it was. Do you think you could give him it with some water once you've got him in bed?"

"Sure" I agree. "But won't he be able to tell the difference?"

"Nah, once he's taken it he'll be out fairly quickly and sleep for hours, he'll never be any the wiser. He needs the rest to heal."

Doc goes off to his room, bringing back the medication for me. I head back to the table to separate Angel from his buddies and get him into bed.

"Come on Angel, let's get you into bed." No sooner have I uttered the words than the catcalls and innuendo start being thrown around by the guys. Honestly.

I give them a look that silences them. Angel doesn't look like he has the energy to make it back to the room at all. I'm not sure how the fuck he even made it here from the hospital. I spot Dragon and call him over.

"Give me a hand Dragon?" I gesture over to Angel and he immediately understands what I'm asking. He moves to stand at Angel's side as I help him rise from the chair, then allows Angel to lean on him as we head back to his room.

I walk in ahead of them, pulling the sheets back from the bed so Angel can lie down. Dragon gets him settled then kisses me on the forehead before leaving the room. "Look after him sweetie."

I smile, giving him a nod in return. Angel just lies on the bed, watching me as I start to remove his boots. When I move higher and start to loosen the waistband on his jeans I can feel him getting hard underneath me, a predatory look on his face.

"Careful what you're doing there Princess." his voice is breaking. He should be resting that throat of his.

I pull his jeans down, removing them and placing them on the chair behind me. I look back up at him, it's obvious how turned on he is: he's sporting a huge erection. It's having an effect on me as well, how could it not, looking at that hard cock?

Holy shit, how the fuck am I supposed to survive this last night sharing his bed?

It's going to break my heart for sure.

Chapter Twenty Five

Eve

I look at Angel and see he's watching me with dark, brooding eyes. "Come here baby."

How can I refuse him?

I remove my jeans and shirt, giggling at Angels groan of approval as I tease him with a slow striptease . I scoot up the bed, gently resting down beside him, careful not to hurt him. Drinking in the sight of him. Fuck this man is sexy. He leans in and kisses me but not before I notice him wince. To save him further pain I lean into him, making sure he's fully lying on his back.

"Straddle me." He demands. I'm not sure this is such a good idea. If I climb on top of him I know what will happen. Fuck it, it's an excellent idea. This can be my way of saying goodbye.

I smile as I do what he's asked. He's always in control, even when he's in pain and unable to move properly, he's still dominant.

We continue to kiss, our tongues dancing, my whimpers the only sound in the room. Angel thrusts his hard erection against me, making me quiver. My arousal deepens. I don't wait for him to tell me what to do. I create a trail of soft teasing kisses down his muscled chest, licking around his belly button and continuing lower. When I get to the waistband of his boxers, I grab either side of them, slowly easing them down. I lick my lips when I reveal his rock hard length. I'm eager to taste him. His cock jerks as I admire it, and I look back up at him. He looks between me and his cock, raising an eyebrow in an unspoken challenge. Naturally I accept, settling myself between his legs.

I lick my way up his length, swirling my tongue around the smooth tip. Just when he thinks I'm going to take him in my mouth I stop, licking my way back down. I keep going down, gently drawing his balls into my mouth and nipping at them with my teeth, drawing a deep groan from Angel. I love to tease him. It makes him impatient to take control, but this time he can't, allowing me the upper hand for a change. I'm tracing my tongue back up his length, repeating my route twice more when Angel thrusts hard against my mouth. "Don't push it Princess."

On a smile I answer. "What's the matter baby?"

His eyes darken. "No more teasing. Suck my cock." I pretend to think it over. "I'll hurt myself if I have to make you." he pouts.

I look at his serious face, realizing he's right. He won't care if he hurts himself, he knows that as well as I do. Damn him for ending my fun. I lean back down slowly, blowing lightly on his swollen tip. "Eve." He warns.

I take him as deep as I can, causing him to drop his head back onto the pillow and moan. "Ah, fuck, yeah baby." I work him in my mouth, taking him as deep as my gag reflex will let me. I suck on the end of his cock, causing him to curse. I love having this control over him. With him wet from my mouth I manage to take him a little deeper. I suck hard as I come back up to the tip, beginning to stroke him up and down at the same time my mouth sucks. "Stop." I keep on. "Eve baby, stop. I'm gonna come but I want to come in your pussy."

Can't argue with that. I'm already naked so I slowly crawl back up his body, sitting astride him. When I'm positioned perfectly over him Angel pushes himself in, barely entering me. I draw in a breath at how good this feels. He thrusts again, this time wincing as he moves. I know he won't admit that he's hurting so I take control. I lower myself so that he fills me inch my delicious inch. I torture myself by going slowly. When I've taken all of him I allow myself a moment to adjust. He's so big that I'm still not completely used to his size yet.

When I'm ready I begin to move. Angel leans in to kiss me. It feels like there's a lot of emotion in this kiss. I don't know what to think. He's probably just making sure I'm enjoying one last great fuck before I go home. Yeah, that sounds right. I want him to feel my emotion too. I pour all of my feelings into the kiss whilst riding his cock. I hold onto his strong jaw, surrendering to the sensations that are now overwhelming me. Our connection has always been strong and I can really feel it tonight.

Our kiss comes to an end, we're staring into each other's eyes, both panting for breath. This is intense. It's just as pleasurable as the hard rough sex we normally enjoy. Not better, just different and on a whole other level.

"Fuck that feels good Princess." Angel growls under me. "That's it, ride my cock."

God I love it when he talks to me like that. His words spur me on. I move faster and harder, taking care to be gentle. I moan as his cock hits my inner wall, creating sparks that will no doubt have me spiraling into my orgasm. I'm in a weird situation right now. My body feels amazing while we're having sex, being this close to Angel is so special to me, but I also feel sad. Even though I'm experiencing these incredible sensations, I feel as if I could cry at the same time.

So that Angel won't see my tears I lean in to kiss him some more. Angel's lips are addictive. I want to remember just how they feel. When I remember him when I'm back home I want to be able to perfectly recall everything about him. Every muscle. Every lick. Every kiss. Every tattoo.

"God I wish I could fuck you so hard right now." Angel complains. I grind against him some more. "I would bend you over and fuck you so hard you'd scream."

I sit up, continuing to move against him. His cock hits the magic spot. I'm taking him so much deeper, I throw my head back. Fuck, that feels so good! "Make those tits bounce for me Princess."

Fuck! Did I mention how much I love his dirty mouth?

My head is thrown back, my eyes closed and my hands are gripping his chiseled waist, trying to stay away from his injured shoulder. I don't see when he reaches over with his good arm and starts teasing my clit. Oh shit that feels good. He continues to torment my clit, showing no mercy. Our eyes lock together. "Come with me." he demands. And I do.

"Fuck, Gabe!" We climax together, my orgasm still rolling through me as we fall together in a sweaty heap.

When I've gathered enough strength I slowly climb off him and head to the bathroom to clean myself up. I bring a damp cloth back to the bed, taking my time gently cleaning my man. I pick up the sedative that Doc gave me. Angel rolls his eyes when I hand it over with a glass of water. "You need painkillers to be able to sleep." I place a soft kiss on his forehead.

He swallows the pill and water as I take a deep breath. I wasn't exactly lying to him.

I climb into bed and he pulls me closer to him. My back to his front, his arms surrounding me. I love spooning and sleeping like this, I'm really going to miss it. I hold back the tears that are threatening to fall. This will be the last time he holds me. I won't see him again.

Gabe

I'm holding Eve as we lie in bed. We've been this way for about ten minutes. I keep thinking about what I need to say and how I should say it.

That was fucking intense sex. I'm proud of my girl for blowing my mind like that. Who knew taking it slow could be just as good as hard sex? Maybe I should let her go on top more often. Then again, I like being in control too much.

I was trying to show her how I felt through the way I held her, looked at her, and kissed her.

"Eve?" She's always so drowsy straight after sex. I hope she's not fallen asleep already.

"Hmm?" I smile, she sounds so fucking cute.

"I need to talk to you Princess." My throat's still sore, but I just manage to rasp the words out.

I'm starting to feel like I'm falling asleep. I need to get this out soon. Eve slowly rolls over, looking at me with her sleepy eyes. Her hair is messy, her face is flushed. She's so damn gorgeous.

I want to tell her everything. I want to explain how I feel, that I want her to stay. I want her to bring Elizabeth over, I'd love to meet her. They can both come live here, we'll find a house together. I don't want my old lady and daughter living in the clubhouse. I want to say these things, but I can't. My body feels weighed down and so tired, my eyes unbelievably heavy.

"Gabe?" I tear my eyes open, I love hearing my name spoken by her.

I look at her beautiful face. "I wanna talk."

My voice sounds odd, it seems to come out of my mouth slowly.

Eve giggles. "Yeah, you said that." She plants kisses on my chest, up my neck and finishes on my jaw.

I try again. "I want you..." But I can't finish. Why can't I fucking talk?

"I want you to..." My words are cut off again.

I suddenly realize what's happening. That wasn't a painkiller Doc gave to Eve. It was a fucking sedative. I should have know he'd so this. He always does it to the brothers when they have to rest in order to heal after as serious injury. He knows we don't want to by laying around healing.

"Doc." I manage to speak out loud. Eve gives me a guilty look. "I'm sorry, he told me it was for the best. You need your rest Gabe." She kisses my cheek, settling back beside me. I want to scream at her that I love her but I can't! It's fucking frustrating!

I want to demand that she goes and gets her baby girl and comes back here to stay with me. I'd protect them both with my life. I don't want her to fucking move on! I don't want any fucker anywhere near her, but I can't get my fucking words out!

Blackness takes over and I fall into a deep and undisturbed sleep.

Eve

I feel bad about giving Angel that sedative now. I hoped tonight he'd have told me how he felt about me. Fuck this, if he won't then I will.

I take a deep breath. "Look, I'm going home tomorrow. I wanted to tell you...Well I know we're nothing serious but I..." I stop and bite my lip. "I love you Gabe."

There's no answer. I realize he's fallen asleep. I smile a tiny sad smile. "It's fine, I didn't expect you to say the words back anyway. I just wanted you to know. I'm going back to Elizabeth tomorrow, I'm going to try to move on. I won't ever forget you."

I hold onto Angel's arm as sleep starts to claim me, silent tears rolling down my face.

Chapter Twenty Six

Eve

Waking up slowly, I feel the heat of another body at my side. Angel looks peaceful, the stress of the last few days seems to be leaving him now. He hasn't woken with nightmares either in the last week which is a bonus. He never has told me what they're about but I leave him to it.

When Angel understood what Doc had given him I felt guilty as fuck. He was right to do it though, Angel would have been in too much pain otherwise, and he's too proud to say anything.

I look at the clock, realizing I have to make a move. It's going to break my heart to leave this man, but I need my daughter more. This isn't a life for her. It wouldn't be fair for me to bring her into the middle of this thing between Angel and me when I don't even know what's happening. My return ticket has me flying home to England in just a few hours. Angel never asked me to stay, we never discussed me going home either, but he knows I'm leaving today. He didn't say anything last night, but that's fine. I didn't really expect him to. To him this was just a casual hook up.

Whilst Teresa and I have re-built our relationship, it will never be quite the same again. I think too much happened between Elvis's death and Teresa's wedding. Certain words were spoken and can't be taken back. Other than the fact I've fallen in love with this man, there's nothing else for me here. Angel made it clear at the start he doesn't do relationships, and as amazing as the sex has been, I don't do casual. I don't like to share. I smile at the thought of seeing Elizabeth, I've missed my baby girl. There were times these past few weeks I never thought I'd get to see her again.

Rising carefully from the bed, wanting to avoid waking my sleeping hero, I head to the shower. The hot water soothes away some of the aches and pains, but I'm not sure I want them all gone. They're a memory of the smoking hot sex I've been enjoying so much of lately. Truth be told, I don't think I'll ever experience sex like that again. I want to hold on to and cherish these memories of Angel.

Pulling my hair into a loose top knot, I wipe the steam from the mirror and examine my face. Despite the hot sex of the past few days I've aged a little. There are lines and creases where there were none before, testament to the nightmare I've lived through. A permanent reminder. I dress slowly, wanting to draw out these last few moments alone with Angel, even if he is sleeping and unaware of my presence. I'll take what I can get.

There's a gentle knock at the door, signalling my time is up. Teresa stands on the other side, pulling me close when she sees the tears falling down my face. "Oh sweetie." She hugs me tight. "It's probably for the best."

She wipes a tear away, only for it to be quickly replaced by a fresh one. "You're making the right decision. You have your baby girl to think about." I know she's right, but at this moment my head and my heart are pulling me in opposite directions. Stepping away from Teresa, I move towards the bed, taking my last memory of Angel as he sleeps. I lean over, gently placing a kiss on his forehead, before turning and grabbing my bags.

As I enter the living area there's a small group of people waiting to see me off. I look over to see Sue, Diane, Dragon, Disney, Ink, Cowboy and even Prez is there. I get passed around as they hug me goodbye. Prez huffs his shoulders and gives me a quick hug, muttering "Take care."

He plants a chaste kiss on my cheek. It's obviously more emotion than he's comfortable showing as I hear him mutter "Fuck it." before quickly heading off in the direction of his office. The others take turns hugging and kissing me again.

Ink gives me an extra long hug. "I'm sorry about all that shit."

"Don't even worry about that." I hug him back, then I'm drawn into a three way hug with Diane and Teresa. There's a few tears shared.

"You better bring that beautiful girl to come and see me." Diane snuffles.

After I agree, they see me safely settled in the driver's seat of my rental car, having loaded my luggage for me. I've declined an escort. Satan's behind bars now so the threat is over. I need this last couple of hours on my own to adjust to my new reality and to maybe shed a few tears in privacy.

The journey back to the airport is uneventful. I return the hire car, moving through check in and boarding on auto pilot. The plane moves along the runway, taking off into a deep blue, cloudless sky. I can't help thinking I've made the wrong decision, but it's too late now. I'm devastated at leaving Angel but I'm so excited about seeing Elizabeth soon.

***

Gabe

I'm woken by the deep, throbbing pain in my shoulder. Fuck! Getting shot hurts.

I reach for Eve, pretty sure she can distract me with that sexy mouth of hers on my cock, just like she did last night. The sheets beside me are cold. I open my eyes to see her side of the bed empty. I don't have a good fucking feeling about this.

Struggling from the bed with only one good arm I reach for my shorts, pulling them on one handed. The clock's showing late afternoon. Doc's sneaky sedative really fucking knocked me out.

Then I see it. An envelope with my name on it is laying on Eve's pillow.

What the fuck!

I curse some more trying to get the envelope open with just my good arm and pull out a handwritten letter. Shit. Tell me this isn't what I think it is.

Gabe

I couldn't bring myself to wake you to say goodbye, you looked so peaceful sleeping. Leaving you is hard enough without having to look you in the eye as I say it. As badly as I want to stay and see where this thing between us is going, I miss my baby girl more.

I've got to be her Mummy, she needs me more right now than you do. Truth be told, I need her just as badly.

I'll never forget the short, but amazing time we've spent together, the memories of you will keep me warm when my bed is cold and lonely. And yes, the sex was fucking hot and the best I'll ever know!

Take care of yourself and thank you for keeping me safe.

Eve

xxx

Fuck! Shit! Fuck!

I reach for the closest thing to me. The alarm clock and smash it against the wall, the broken pieces falling to the floor.

I can't remember what time her fucking flight was, so head out of the room in search of Teresa. She'll know, and with any luck I'll get to the airport before she leaves and fix this.

I reach the living area and don't understand what I'm seeing. Prez is cursing under his breath, Teresa is sobbing loudly and everyone looks like their dog just died. "What the fucks going on?" I question.

Prez looks up at me. Suddenly I don't want to know. The look on his face is scaring the shit out of me, Teresa's cries have gotten louder since she caught sight of me.

"Satan..." Prez stumbles with his speech. "Satan's out."

What the fuck?

How on earth is he out of jail so quickly?

"There was a fuck up on the paperwork, his bastard of a lawyer got him out on a technicality."

"Fuck, I need to get to the airport now!" I almost collapse to the floor, I'm in so much pain right now but I can't risk losing Eve.

***

The ride to the airport was hell, my shoulder felt every jar and bump in the road. Doc dosed me up on painkillers before we left. Cowboy's driven here like a bat out of hell. We're lucky he didn't get stopped for speeding the way he flew along some of those roads.

We pull up at the drop off for departures, Cowboy helping me out of the vehicle then running back to go park. I enter the airport, where the fuck do I start looking for her.

Spotting the British Airways flight desk I pull the flight details from my pocket. Teresa had them ready for me as we set off in the truck.

The blonde assistant behind the desk looks me up and down, obviously not liking what she sees judging from the sneer on her face.

"How may I help you, sir". Fucking bitch. I hand over the flight details and she takes them slowly. Why the fuck can't she hurry up, does she not realize how important this is to me right now.

"I'm sorry sir, that flight has just departed." She gives me an odd look. "Funny that, I could have sworn I already checked you in."

I crumple to the ground in agony, I'm too late. Eve has left me. That's where Cowboy finds me.

"I'm too late" I sob into his shoulder as he tries to help me stand.

"Don't you dare give up Angel!" he chastises. "We'll sort this, I promise. That's what brothers are for." We limp back to the truck together. He's right, we'll sort this and I will get Eve back. We reach the truck, ready to head back to the clubhouse. My brothers will help me work a plan out.

I lay back against the seat, defeated for now. "I love you Eve, don't worry Princess, you're mine, and I'm coming to claim what's mine."

Epilogue

Satan

I owe my lawyer big time, the fucker came through for me. I don't know who he had to pay off, but the paperwork went to fuck and I'm back on the streets.

I grab my bag, throwing it over my shoulder as I walk into the huge building.

I see my target ahead of me, she hasn't a clue I'm here. Stupid bitch can't see anything for all the fucking tears she's wasting. This is sweet.

I keep out of her line of vision just to be sure, I don't want my surprise spoiling yet.

***

The door closes behind me, I'm the last one through. Still she can't see me, her heads bowed down, probably fucking crying again, stupid bitch.

I take my seat, scaring the shit out of the old lady at my side. I love the effect my cut has on people.

I settle back, I'm in for a long haul but this is going to be so sweet. I know my fucker of a brother set me up. Well now I'm going to pay him back, big time.

A voice comes over the tannoy "Good afternoon ladies and gentlemen. This is your captain speaking. Welcome to flight BA0016 bound for London Heathrow. We hope you enjoy your flight with us today."

I look ahead of me, Eve sits several rows ahead, totally unaware that I'm here on the same plane as her.

I've never been to England before, I'm quite looking forward to it. But, I'm looking forward to having some one on one time with Eve even more.

To be continued...

Acknowledgements

To our amazing team of beta readers who swore at us, cried with us and generally kept us on the straight and narrow - Diane, Elle, Angi, Margreet, Mandy and Amy - thank you, we couldn't have done this without your support.

To the bloggers who shared in our cover reveal, release blitz and book tour, you play such an important part in bringing authors and writers together, thank you.

To the authors we love and who feed our passion for books, there are too many to name and we'd hate to leave one of you out, but please know how important you are to us. You inspire us.

About K.T Fisher

I love reading, it's my favourite hobby. I've always had ideas for my own books packed into my head so I thought I would write them out for people to enjoy

Stalk K.T. Fisher

Facebook:

https://www.facebook.com/pages/KTFisher/490003474414733?ref=ts&fref=ts

Twitter: @KTFisher_Author

Goodreads: https://www.goodreads.com/KTFisher

About Ava Manello

I'm a passionate reader, blogger, publisher, and author. I love nothing more than helping other Indie authors publish their books - be that reviewing, beta reading, formatting or proofreading,

I love erotic suspense that's well written and engages the reader, and I love promoting the heck out of it over on my book blog

http://www.kinkybookklub.co.uk

Stalk Ava Manello

Facebook: http://www.facebook.com/avamanello

Twitter: @AvaManello

Goodreads: https://www.goodreads.com/AvaManello

Website: http://www.avamanello.co.uk

Printed in Great Britain
by Amazon